BOOKED FOR CHRISTMAS

A MISTLETOE MOUNTAIN NOVEL

MELISSA F. MILLER

BROWN STREET BOOKS

To my mom

PLAYLIST

Here's a collection of songs to listen to while you read *Home for Christmas in July*. Find a cozy corner, add your favorite beverage, and you'll be all set. You can also find the playlist on my website, melissafmiller.com.

"Winter Song," Leslie Odom, Jr.
"Winter," Joshua Radin
"Blue Christmas," Rod Stewart
"Last Christmas," Clementine Duo
"A Holly Jolly Christmas," Lady A
"Kiss Me," Sixpence None The Richer
"Let It Snow," She & Him
"On this Winter's Night," Lady A
"BIRDS OF A FEATHER," Billie Eilish
"Merry Christmas," Ed Sheeran, Elton John

"Merry Christmas Baby," Colbie Caillat, Brad Paisley

"All I Want for Christmas Is You," Clementine Duo

"Love You for a Long Time," Maggie Rogers

"Maybe this Christmas," Tyler Shaw

"Simply the Best," Noah Reid

"Love Is Christmas," Sara Bareilles

"I Think They Call this Love," Matthew Ifield

"Glittery," Kacey Musgraves, Troye Sivan

"A Marshmallow World," Clementine Duo

"Can't Help Falling in Love," Haley Reinhart

"Mistletoe," Colbie Caillat

"Hold on Forever," Rob Thomas

"I'm Yours," Jason Mraz

"Winter Wonderland," Laufey

"invisible string," Taylor Swift

"Die with a Smile," Lady Gaga, Bruno Mars

"Snow Day," Caitlyn Smith

"Maybe this Christmas," Michael Bublé, Carly Pearce

"Hard Candy Christmas," Dolly Parton

"Christmas Lights," Coldplay

"Anthem," Father John Misty

"Call It Dreaming," Iron & Wine

"Christmas Isn't Christmas," Dan + Shay

"Under the Tree," Sam Palladio

"Cold December Night," Michael Bublé

"Holiday Party," Dan + Shay
"Falling," Oh Gravity

CHAPTER 1

A SUGAR BOMB SPIT TAKE

Holly

I join the line of caffeine seekers snaking through the Snowflake Cafe and pull out my phone to check the time. I started my morning early and set the tone for the day with a long run, some yoga, and a short meditation. As a result, I am centered, I am calm, I am … absolutely, positively going to freaking scream if this line doesn't start moving faster.

Breathe.

I breathe. My irritation continues to rise as the line inches forward in slow motion. How can I be this irritated at seven in the morning? The day hasn't even really begun yet. This doesn't bode well for me. I tap through my emails on my phone—more to distract me from the Christmas music blaring from the cafe's speakers than out of any need to get work done.

It's going to be a slow work day, as the day after Thanksgiving should be. I have no court appearances, and most of my coworkers plan to work from home or take the entire day off. The office will be quiet. It's the perfect opportunity to dig out from under the mountain of paperwork on my desk and ease into the weekend feeling accomplished and organized. Assuming I don't snap from the music and lack of coffee first.

I'm not surprised Delphina's playing holiday music. When you live in a town named Mistletoe Mountain, it's a given that Christmas is a big deal. The festivities are out of control all year round, to be fair. But Mistletoe Mountain really ramps it up the moment folks prepare to flip their calendars from November to December. It's as if someone has let a racehorse out of a pen—or released the contestants in a timed grocery store cart-filling game show. Wild abandon.

I remind myself of the *Dhamma* talk I recently heard about sitting with your pain. Acknowledge it, don't resist it —that was the gist. Would the same principle work with extreme, bordering on murderous, aggravation? No time like the present to give it a try.

I close my eyes and acknowledge Mariah Carey's incredible vocal range and undisputed lyrical economy while pretending my skin doesn't itch. Or am I supposed to be one with the itching? Maybe I'm doing this all wrong.

I open my eyes as the song switches over. While George Michael is giving me his heart, I finally reach the front of the line.

"Holly!" Delphina smiles broadly, bouncing along to the music, which makes her metallic Christmas ornament earrings jangle.

"Hi, Delph. Nice earrings," I say gamely.

Either my barely hidden disdain sails over my best friend's head or, more likely, she chooses to ignore it.

"Thanks. What can I get you?"

I raise an eyebrow. "The same as always. A large black coffee to go, two suspended coffees, and two suspended meals."

I hand over my reusable Snowflake Cafe stainless steel tumbler, which I use to help the environment (and get my fifty-cent discount) despite the cutesy pastel snowflake design that graces the thing. Humming a Christmas song—*not* the one streaming through the speakers, mind you— she takes an inordinately long time to pour coffee into a travel mug.

At last, she returns and slides it across the counter. "Busy day?"

"Yeah, I guess. I don't know," I mumble as I tap my card against the reader.

She rests her elbows on the counter and peers at me. I know what's coming, and I should have planned for it, should have had a ready excuse to deflect it. But I didn't, so

I'm going to have to wing it. Think on my feet, as my new boss likes to say.

"Are you going to the Christmas tree lighting tonight?"

"I can't. I have to work."

"On Black Friday?"

"You're working," I point out.

She purses her lips.

"What?" I demand, even though I know better.

"Your dad sponsors the lighting."

"Right, so the family is well represented. Besides, my sisters and Noelle will be there. They wouldn't dream of missing it." I flash her my brightest, fakest smile.

"Yeesh, don't grimace like that," she orders. "You look like you're about to go on a killing spree. Don't you want to see the tree light up? It's so pretty."

"It *is* pretty, and I'll get to see it all lit up when I'm on my way home from work."

"Well, I'm going to save you a spot under the gazebo, just in case you change your mind."

In response to this promise (or is it a threat?), I give my best friend since second grade a genuinely warm smile—hopefully one that doesn't make me look homicidal. "Don't hold your breath."

She sighs, shakes her head, and starts wiping down the counter with more vigor than is strictly necessary.

As I head for the door, two things happen. One, I take a sip of my black coffee, and my taste buds are assaulted as a sugar bomb explodes in my mouth. Two, the doors of the coffee shop open with a loud jingle of bells and someone steps inside. I react instinctively to the taste in my mouth and spew the offending liquid. The alleged 'coffee' splashes all over an argyle sweater stretched across an impressively broad male chest.

"Oh my goodness, I'm so sorry!" I yelp.

The man just inside the doorway laughs huskily and futilely tries to brush away the coffee with his hands.

Delphina rushes around from behind the counter with a damp rag and starts dabbing at him.

"What's in here?" I shake the tumbler accusatorially. "This is not my coffee order."

She's still fussing over the guy when she eyes me cautiously from under her elf hat and confesses, "It's a gingerbread latte with candy cane foam. I thought you could use a little holiday spirit."

"You thought I could use a little tooth decay? Black coffee, Delph. Black. Coffee. You know that's my order."

She waves a dismissive hand at me and returns to blotting the liquid dessert out of the sweater.

I turn back to the stranger, who stands there with a bemused expression, watching this play out. "I'm so sorry. Let me buy you a coffee."

He smiles a crooked smile. "No need. I'll just go to the men's room and take care of this."

"It's that way." Delphina points down the hall to the bathrooms, and he heads off.

He can't possibly be out of earshot, when she grabs my arm and squeals, "He's hot!"

I scrunch up my forehead. "I guess."

"You guess?"

"Yeah, I guess. I was distracted by the insulin shock. I didn't really check him out," I lie.

She starts listing his attributes. "Shaggy sandy blond hair. Big, soulful blue eyes. Broad shoulders. Sexy scruff. A toe-tingling smile."

"He does have a good smile," I agree. "You should ask him out."

She gives me a blank look. "No, dummy. You should ask him out."

"Me? You're the one salivating over him."

"First of all, he's not my type."

I'll give her that. Delphina likes bad boys—tattoos, motorcycles, piercings. Argyle sweater man is not her jam. He's also not *my* type. From the glimpse I caught, he struck me as outdoorsy. I'll bet he tent camps and works for a nonprofit, not that any of that's *bad,* mind you. But I'm drawn to clean-cut men in well-cut suits.

She's still talking, "Second of all, you're the one who had the meet cute."

"The meet cute?" I echo, bewildered.

"The amusing first meeting that you can tell your grandchildren about someday."

"I spat on him," I remind her.

"Exactly!"

"Third, you haven't dated since you called off your engagement with—"

I hold up my hand to stave her off. "Don't say his name. You already tried to poison me. I don't think I can take a dagger to the heart, too."

For a moment, she's silent, and I think I have her.

But she knows me too well. She shakes her head. "You're not pining for Anderson. You're just *wallowing*. What I can't figure out is why."

I ignore this and sigh. "I have to go to work. Don't let that guy pay for his coffee, okay? Just let me know how much he spends, and I'll transfer it to you."

"Or you could just give it to me at the tree lighting," she calls after me.

I pretend not to hear her as I hurry out of the cafe. Once I round the corner and am sure I'm out of eyesight from the cafe, I take the lid off my mug and pour the sugary concoction down the sewer grate. Just as the last drops of the vile liquid vanish into the opening, one of the county sheriff's cruisers comes into view. I freeze, holding my breath. Is it illegal dumping to pour coffee—or whatever this stuff is—into the sewer system?

As I search my memory for an applicable law or regulation—and more importantly, a defense thereto—the black and white hits its lights and siren and speeds past me. I exhale and return the lid to my mug. Then I pick up my pace as I head for my car because now I need to make another stop to find a cup of actual coffee before I start my workday.

CHAPTER 2

I WANT AN ATTORNEY

Jack

Igrab an unbleached paper towel from the pile on the sink vanity and wet it. I spend about a minute making a halfhearted attempt to blot at the brown stain spreading across the front of my sweater, then shrug, wad up the compostable towel, and pitch it into the basket. The stain'll come out or it won't. At least it blends with the forest green and brown pattern. I think.

I push the door open and walk out into the little coffee shop's front area. During my brief attempt at repairs, the line at the counter has somehow grown exponentially.

As I weave through the crowd, making my way to the end of the queue, the elf behind the counter leans across it, waving her arms. "Yo! Yo, beardy guy!"

"Me?" I jab a thumb toward my chest.

"Yes, you. Don't get in that line. Come to the front."

"No, no, that's okay. I don't need—"

"Make way, people. Bearded stranger coming through!" Her clear voice cuts through the overlapping conversations and the holiday music.

I cast a cautious glance toward the line but no one seems ready to mutiny. Instead, the crowd parts to create room for me to pass through. As they comply with the elf's commands, they keep up a steady stream of loud chatter about a Christmas tree lighting. The majority of the patrons seem to be wearing holiday sweaters, and I spy several Santa hats.

I sidle past a tall, austere woman wearing a warm-up jacket with Maple Twist Fitness embroidered across the back and present myself at the counter.

"Sorry," I mumble.

"Oh no. Go right ahead," she says with an encouraging nod that sets the reindeer antlers on her headband bobbing.

The woman behind the counter flashes a grateful smile. "Thanks for understanding, Griselda. Our friend here was the victim of a splash and run."

"No damage done," I assure her, gesturing toward my chest.

"So what'll it be?" she chirps.

I study the board behind her. "You know, I planned to get a cup of tea but whatever that Grinch spilled on me smells really good. I'll have that instead."

"One gingerbread latte with candy cane foam coming right up. If you buy a reusable tumbler, you get a discount on refills."

I start to shake my head, about to explain that I'm just passing through town, when the tall woman behind me leans forward. "You should get one. I swear they're magic. They keep drinks hot all day."

I still have a long road trip ahead of me. A reliable insulated mug would be better than continuing to collect disposable cups as I rack up miles.

"Sure, why not."

The woman clamps a strong hand on my shoulder. "Good choice."

"Any particular color?" The elf asks, sweeping a hand over a neat row of shiny stainless steel travel mugs.

"Surprise me."

She plucks a mug from the middle of the line then turns away to prepare the drink. She returns a moment later and places the snowflake-festooned tumbler on the counter in front of me.

I pull out my worn wallet. "What do I owe you?"

"Oh no, Holly took care of it."

"Holly?"

"The Grinch," she says with a twinkle in her eye.

"Oh, no. That's not necessary."

She waves her hand. "It's fine. Honestly, she said she'd cover whatever you get. So if you want a cookie or croissant, you might as well live it up."

I frown. "I don't want to take advantage. At least charge me for the tumbler."

"Nope." She folds her arms over her chest. The woman behind me snorts.

I know better than to battle with a woman whose mind is made up, so I pluck a ten from the dwindling stack of cash in my billfold and start to shove it into the tip jar. The elf stops me with a hand on my arm.

"I appreciate the tip, but if you're so inclined you could pay for a suspended coffee or sandwich instead."

I throw her a blank look, and she points to a large cork board hanging on the wall to my right. I turn my head and scan a colorful calendar of community events—there are *a lot* of them. Then my eyes slide to the dozens of red and green slips of paper pinned to the board alongside the calendar. The row of red slips list beverages—I see 'large coffee,' 'hot chocolate,' 'tea or chai,' and 'latte' at a glance. The green slips are all foods—things like sandwiches, salads, and cookies.

Understanding sets in before she begins her explanation. "If you buy a suspended food or a drink, it goes up on the board until someone who needs one pulls the slip down. No questions asked."

"That's a great idea," I tell her as I stuff the ten into the tip jar.

Disappointment flashes in her brown eyes and her smile falters.

Then I remove a twenty from my wallet and pass it over

the counter to her. "Put this toward whatever people are most likely to need."

The smile returns. "Thank you."

I raise my new travel mug and tip it toward her. Then I take my first sip of the hot, sweet drink. It tastes exactly like a gingerbread cookie topped with peppermint frosting. "This is great. The Grinch doesn't know what she's talking about."

"That one's my fault," she tells me. "I know Holly doesn't like frou-frou coffee drinks."

The woman in line behind me cracks, "She always says she takes it black and strong, like her heart."

Both women chuckle.

"Still," I say, shaking my head, "I can't imagine why a person who hates Christmas would live in a town called Mistletoe Mountain."

The chuckles turn into full-bodied chortles.

"She doesn't hate Christmas," the elf tells me. "Her family owns the inn. The Jollys love the holidays more than anyone—and in this town, that's saying something. Holly just hates *this* Christmas."

The woman behind me mutters something I don't catch under her breath.

It feels as if an apology is in order. "I shouldn't judge. Sometimes the holidays are hard."

"Sometimes they are."

"Well, tell Holly I said thanks for the drink."

"I will." She flicks her eyes toward the cork board. I

follow her gaze to a flyer announcing a Christmas tree lighting in the town square. When I turn back to her, she's grinning. "If you're still in town tonight, you should come to the Christmas tree lighting. And you can thank Holly yourself. You know, the suspended meals and drinks were her idea," she adds this last sentence out of nowhere.

Before I can respond, the jingle bells over the door jangle loudly as the door opens and two police officers plow through the crowd of caffeine seekers.

"Is the owner of the red station wagon with Florida plates in here?" the male officer booms in a commanding voice.

The room falls silent, save for the rendition of 'Have Yourself A Merry Little Christmas' piping through the cafe's speakers.

I step forward. "That's me."

"Sir, we're going to need you to come with us," the female officer says, her hand resting on the handcuffs dangling from her hip.

"Did I park illegally?" I'm sure I didn't.

The elf leans over the counter and addresses the male officer. "What's going on, Ned?"

"Nothing to worry about, Delphina. Sir," he jerks his chin toward me.

"Come on, Liza," the Maple Twist lady presses the female officer, who shakes her head.

"Stay out of it, Gris."

I follow them outside. As soon as my feet hit the pavement, I'm up against the wall. Officer Ned takes my tumbler as Officer Liza snaps the handcuffs around my wrists.

"I don't understand—" I begin.

She cuts me off and reads off a laminated card. "You have the right to remain silent. Anything you say can and will be used against you in a court of law. You have the right to an attorney. If you cannot afford an attorney, one will be provided for you. Do you understand these rights?"

I swallow hard. "I do. And I want an attorney."

CHAPTER 3

SCREAMING IN THE CAR

Holly

Thanks to Delphina's sugar bomb assault, I'm forced to drive to the diner in Stonebridge for my coffee on my way to the office. The public defender's office where I work is in the valley, not in Mistletoe Mountain proper, so at least the Christmas contagion is diluted here. The only concessions to the holiday in the diner are a ceramic tabletop Christmas tree with multicolored old-fashioned mini-lightbulbs aglow next to the cash register and the container of my sister Merry's peppermint candies beside it.

I'm patiently waiting for my to-go cup of blessedly bitter, dark coffee when my phone chimes. I glance at the notification bar. It's a text from Delphina. I swipe it open, expecting to see either an apology for the abomination she tried to pass off as my coffee order or more nagging about attending the Christmas tree lighting. To my surprise, it's neither. Instead, she's written:

> OMG! You missed the excitement right after you left. Call me when you get a chance.

Call her? She's usually way too busy to talk on the phone when she's at her shop. Especially in the mornings. Not to mention, who talks on the phone anymore? So whatever she has to tell me must be juicy. I'm just about to hit the icon to call her when I hear my name.

I lift my head to see Roslyn Porter waving and grinning broadly at me. She clatters across the linoleum floor on her high-heeled shoes. "Am I glad to see you, Holly."

"Morning, Roz," I say cautiously.

Roz is always working, even when she isn't working. So her unbridled joy at seeing me isn't as flattering as it might seem. She takes exactly one breath before revealing why she's so happy to run into me.

"The judge was assigned a criminal case this morning. It just came in."

I steel myself to tell her I can't help her, but she plows ahead.

"The defendant is an out-of-towner. The district attorney's office wants to hold him without bail because they think he's a flight risk."

We both roll our eyes. There aren't many crimes

committed in Mistletoe Mountain and the surrounding towns, and almost none that require holding the defendant without bail.

"Roz—," I begin.

"You know he's going to end up being assigned to your office anyway. Let's chalk one up for efficiency."

Roz is a force of nature, and, while, sure I can argue with her, she's right—I'll just be delaying the inevitable. So I save my breath and sigh instead. "What time's the hearing?"

"Well, since you're already here, we can push it up. As a courtesy." She grins.

Stonebridge is the county seat, and the courthouse is located right on the town square, less than a mile from where we stand.

"I haven't even been into the office yet, Roz."

"Perfect, don't go in. That way you won't get waylaid with other cases and people needing things from you. Just grab your coffee and come straight to the courthouse."

As she says this, Betty appears at the counter with two takeout coffees. I take one while Roz snags the other.

"I'll see you in a few," I say.

"I just need Betty to box up my donuts," she says loud enough for Betty to hear and put a little hustle in her step. "I take them in every Friday for the courthouse staff. You know, everybody likes to end the work week on a sweet note."

I'm beginning to suspect that this entire county is

controlled by a cartel of dentists. I just nod, eager to get outside and call Delphina to find out what's so important before I plunge into my new case.

"By the way—," Roz begins just as I reach the door. Her overly casual tone makes my chest tighten. I turn around and eye her. "I might not have mentioned that Anderson Carson is the assistant district attorney handling this case. See you at the courthouse!"

I gape at her as my face heats. I can't face Anderson. Not now. The primary reason I plan to hibernate during the month-long holiday celebration that takes over the entire town is to *avoid Anderson.* It's literally written on my goal list for the month under self-care: A. A., Avoid Anderson.

Having a case against him will ensure I don't meet this crucial goal. I open my mouth and she tilts her head. It's not a head tilt that says, 'I understand if you need to reconsider.' It's more of a 'Are you really going to tell a judge you can't take a representation because your love life fell apart?' head tilt.

She's right. I nod, clamp my mouth closed to swallow the string of swear words rising in my throat, then wheel back around and push the door open with more force than necessary. I speed-walk to my car, launch myself into the driver's seat, and rest my head against the steering wheel, letting out a strangled scream as I do so.

That feels good, so I scream louder. Then I lift my head, throw it back, and shriek. It's a raw, wordless expression of rage and frustration. But it feels powerful and freeing, unlike all the sobbing I indulged in over the summer.

I pull down the visor mirror and address my reflection aloud in a voice made raspy by all the screaming, "I am a warrior. I can do this. I *will* do this."

Pep talk completed, I start the car and call Delphina through my Bluetooth connection. Not surprisingly, my call rolls to voicemail. I leave a brief message:

"Hey, I got your text but couldn't call you until now. I've been corralled into doing a bail hearing, so I'll be in court for the rest of the morning. Oh, and *Anderson* is representing the county." I pause for the shriek of indignation I know this news will elicit from my best friend. "Of course, this is all *your* fault because I ran into the judge's secretary at the diner—where I was getting a cup of real coffee. Talk to you later."

I don't *really* blame Delph. If Roz hadn't collared me at the diner, she'd have called the public defender's office. And as the newest lawyer, odds are I'd have been asked to take the case even if I weren't the only person in the office today. But, still, I can't believe I'm about to go toe-to-toe in court with the one person I desperately want to avoid during the month-long Christmas extravaganza that takes over Mistletoe Mountain. Anderson Wilson Carson, Esquire, hotshot assistant district attorney on the rise, permanent entry on the Naughty List, and my adulterous ex-fiancé.

CHAPTER 4

A REAL SON OF A BLITZEN

Jack

I don't know how long I've been sitting in the cell at the police station. There's a clock on the wall, but it's out of my line of vision, whether by design or happenstance. There's no one else in here. Just me in this big, surprisingly clean box with a long bench built into one wall.

I sit and I wait. It's almost relaxing. No notifications dinging on my phone, nowhere to be, no one to answer to. The only noise is the distant hum of conversation from the squad room and the occasional bark of laughter.

It's a luxury to simply lose myself in my thoughts. Well, it would be if my current thoughts were something other than I have no idea why I've been arrested and I really hope this town has a defense attorney who can get me out of this so that the rest of my trip doesn't get derailed.

As if I've summoned an attorney with this thought, Officer Liza appears around the corner, her hands on her hips.

"Let's go, Mr. Bell. That attorney you wanted is here." She puts an old-fashioned key in the lock, and the bars swing open.

I step forward, then stop, unsure of the protocol. Can I walk right out? Or do I need to wait for her to handcuff me?

She raises an eyebrow. "You don't want to come?"

"I wasn't sure if you need to handcuff me first." I hold my wrists out in front of me.

She rolls her eyes. "The handcuffing was a little dramatic," she tells me. "But Ned insisted, and he's got seniority."

"I'm not dangerous," I assure her.

"I figured as much. Just don't prove me wrong by taking a swing at your counsel." She gestures for me to walk out.

I do, and she leads me down a bright hallway. She stops in front of the last door and knocks once. Without waiting for a response, she pushes it open.

"He's all yours," she announces.

My attorney stands up from the far side of a metal table.

I do a double take. "You?" I ask.

"You?" she answers, wide-eyed.

The police officer chuckles to herself as she backs out into the hall and pulls the door closed.

The woman on the other side of the table continues to gape at me. My court-appointed lawyer is none other than the cranky blonde from the Snowflake Cafe who doused me in coffee. She blinks her clear blue eyes, once, twice, brushes a tendril of hair back from her face, and then steps forward and extends her hand.

"I'm H. Evelyn Jolly. I work for the public defender's office. I've been assigned to represent you, Mr. Bell."

"Please, call me Jack," I tell her as I take her warm hand in mine as she gives me a brisk shake. Then I tilt my head. "I thought your name was Holly."

Her brow wrinkles. "I don't remember telling you my name."

"You didn't, but Delphina at the coffee shop and a very tall, fit woman in line behind me did."

She twists her mouth into a knowing bow. "Was this tall woman wearing a warm-up suit?"

I nod. "The jacket said Maple Twist Fitness."

"That's Griselda. What else did those two tell you?"

I think for a moment. "That you take your coffee like your heart."

"Black and strong," she confirms. Then she adds, as an afterthought, "And bitter."

I cock my head and continue, "They also said you aren't the holiday-hater you appear to be."

She shrugs and lets that pass.

"So, your name *is* Holly?"

A heavy sigh. "Yes, my name is Holly."

"Holly Jolly?" I try to suppress a snicker and fail.

She jabs a finger at me. "And *this* is why I go by H. Evelyn in court."

"It's … cute."

"Yeah, adorable," she deadpans.

"I didn't mean to laugh," I tell her sincerely. "I'm sorry."

She dismisses my apology with a chop of her hand. "Forget about it. You're hardly the first person to find it funny. But we don't have time for this. We have an arraignment in about twenty minutes. I need you to tell me what exactly happened."

I shake my head. "I have no idea. I ordered a coffee—the one you, uh, spat on me, as a matter of fact. It smelled so good, I decided to get one. I tried to pay, but Delphina refused to take my money. She said you covered it. Thank you, by the way."

"It was the least I could do. Please continue."

I search my memory. "I put some money in the suspended meals jar and took my coffee. We chatted about how your family owns an inn and is big into the holidays. Then Delphina suggested I stick around town to go to the Christmas tree lighting tonight."

She snorts. "Of course she did."

"I was about to leave when two police officers came in and asked if the owner of a red station wagon with Florida plates was in the building. I said that was me, and they asked me to step outside. The male officer took my drink, and the female officer handcuffed me. I didn't even get to drink my coffee." I give a rueful shake of my head.

"You've gotta stop calling that coffee. Believe me, you didn't miss anything."

I laugh despite myself. "I told them I wanted an attorney and we drove to the station in silence. I genuinely have no idea what they think I did."

She sighs and glances down at a sheet of paper in her hand. "What they think you did, Jack, was criminal trespass. That's what they're planning to charge you with."

"Trespass? That's impossible. What does it say? Where did I trespass?"

"It's not on this intake sheet, and I really don't want to find out in court, so please try to remember everywhere you went. When did you get into town?"

"Early this morning. I'm just passing through."

"What did you do before you went to the Snowflake Cafe?"

"I stopped for gas. As I was pulling out of the gas station I saw a sign declaring a place called Snow Lake the best spot in town to watch the sunrise. I'm not really in a hurry, so I drove over there." I pause. "Do you know where I'm talking about?"

"Yes. My family owns a cabin on the other side of the lake. And the sunrise usually is spectacular."

"It was," I agree. "I was there for a while, watching the swans glide around. When I left, I decided to stop in town and get a coffee for the road." I lift my hands and shrug.

"You didn't stop anywhere else before you came to the coffee shop?"

"No."

She frowns. "And you went straight from the gas station to the lake? You're sure?"

I search my memory, retracing my steps. "Yes. Wait, no. I did make a stop, but that can't be what this is about."

She holds my gaze, waiting.

"When I was driving to the lake, the sun hadn't risen but the was sky was beginning to lighten. You know? Dawn, I guess. And I noticed a little free library in the front of a home. It was lit by a spotlight, so it caught my eye. I've been adding books to little free libraries all along the East Coast on my trip. Mistletoe Mountain wasn't one of my planned stops, but I was here, so I stopped and put a few books in the box."

"Where is this home?"

"It's outside of the town proper. A big, sprawling rancher on the right side of the road to the lake. There's a pair of stone lions flanking the driveway."

She groans. It's a long, pained sound.

"What?"

"That's the Swansons' place."

"And?"

"Mrs. Swanson can be … difficult. Did you step on her property?"

I throw her a baffled look. "Yeah? I mean, I had to. The library box is in the middle of a garden with a stepping stone path. I parked, got some books out of my trunk, and put them in the library. Then I went on my way."

"You didn't take any books?"

"No."

"Good. She probably would have had you charged with theft, too."

I pause and consider how to ask this question without offending her. "Do you understand how a little free library works?"

"I do. I'm not entirely certain Mrs. Swanson does."

"This is ludicrous."

"It is," she agrees.

"So we can clear this up really easily, right? Can't you just talk to the DA and explain this is all a misunderstanding?" It seems easy enough to me.

She gives me a pained smile. After a moment, she straightens her shoulders and takes a deep breath. "We should be able to resolve this in no time."

"Why do I hear a but?"

"Because there is one."

"I'm all ears."

"The assistant district attorney who authorized your arrest a real son of a Blitzen," she says.

I blink, confused. "A what?"

She throws back her head and laughs at my puzzlement. She has a nice laugh, throaty. Almost a purr of pleasure. I stop my mind before it can go any further down this line of thought and focus on what she's saying.

"It's how we swear around town. You'll get used to it."

"I don't know my reindeer lore, but son of a Blitzen sounds bad."

"It's not great," she admits. "Anderson is a win-at-all-costs guy."

"Anderson?"

"The district attorney. Anderson Wilson Carson."

I laugh. I can't help it. "That's a mouthful."

"They're family names." She shakes her head. "The problem is, Anderson has political ambitions. He might want to make an example out of you."

I stare at her for a long moment, sure I've misheard her. "Make an example out of me *for donating books?*"

She nods unhappily. "It's a possibility."

"What about the judge?"

"Judge MacIntosh is fair," she assures me.

Relieved, I shrug. "Okay, so I'll pay a fine if that's what I have to do to be on my way."

"Let's not get ahead of ourselves. We're going to go upstairs."

"What's upstairs?"

"The courthouse is attached to this police department. And the district attorney's offices are on the other side. All three buildings are connected by long hallways."

"Bet that's convenient during Vermont winters."

She laughs. "It is. Anyway, we're going to find Assistant

District Attorney Carson before arraignment court starts and see if we can't work this out without even involving the judge."

She sounds crisp and confident, but a worry line creases her forehead. There's something she's not telling me.

But I just nod. "Sounds like a plan."

She hits the door with the side of her fist. Officer Liza must be waiting on the other side because the door swings open almost instantly.

"Going up to see Anders?" The police officer shoots my lawyer a look I can't decipher.

"Anders?" Holly parrots.

Liza snorts. "Haven't you heard? He's shortened his name. He wants us all to call him Anders."

"And elves in the North Pole want hot cocoa."

The officer's laughter trails us down the hallway to a stairwell and doesn't fade until Holly pushes open the door and we head upstairs.

CHAPTER 5

UGH. ANDERSON.

Holly

I lead my bewildered client through the warren of hallways that attach the police station to the courthouse and then up a narrow staircase that leads to the DA's offices. There are lawyers who don't even know these three buildings connect, but as a former assistant district attorney, I know all the ins and outs, nooks and crannies, and shortcuts.

I hang a sharp right with Jack on my heels and push open an unmarked door. We emerge in the hallway behind the lobby of the district attorney's office. As we circle around to the front of the reception desk, Chantal Taylor greets me with a genuine smile.

"Holly Jolly, long time, no see."

"Hey, Chantal," I reply warmly. "Is Anderson around?"

One eyebrow shoots up to her hairline. I hurry to explain so she doesn't get the wrong idea. "I have a case with him. I've been assigned to represent Mr. Bell in the criminal trespass case." I gesture to Jack, who gives Chantal a friendly wave.

"Oh?" She draws out the syllable. "That's … something."

"It's something, all right," I agree. "Is he here?"

She gives a nod. As she taps a candy cane-striped fingernail to buzz his office, she informs me he wants us to call him Anders.

"So I've been told."

"Anders, opposing counsel for the criminal trespass is here to see you."

I note that she didn't tell him it was me, and I'm glad. I'd like to have the element of surprise for this conversation.

She nods and hangs up the phone. "He said to show you and your client to Conference Room B and he'll be there in a few minutes. I assume I don't need to show you the way."

She gives me a pained smile and I know she's realized the hallway that leads to Conference Room B will take me right past the supply closet where my love life fell apart. During the office Christmas in July party last summer, I opened the closet to grab more swizzle sticks for the bartender and found Anderson and our boss half-naked and exploring each other's tonsils.

"I like your nails," I tell her, both because I do and because it forestalls any discussion of Anderson's very public betrayal.

She waggles them at me. "Thanks. Hey, Holly?"

"Yeah?" I turn.

"I hope you jingle his bells," she stage whispers.

I'm not entirely sure the euphemism holds up but I appreciate the sentiment. I suppress a laugh and give Chantal a wink. "Thanks."

I turn and lead Jack toward the conference room.

"See you at the tree lighting!" she calls. I wave my hand without turning around.

My cheeks burn as I pass the closet. I'm dreading seeing Anderson, but at least there's no danger of running into Tabitha Waterson. The district attorney famously drives into Burlington for a marathon day of shopping on Black Friday. In fact, I'm surprised Anderson didn't go with her. Last I heard, Anderson and Tabitha were still together.

But then, I'm not exactly in the loop on the office gossip. After my humiliation at the party, I couldn't bear to work with the two of them, so I resigned. Our family attorney, Marley Jacobs, offered me a job as an associate. I almost took it. And maybe, someday, I'll join her. But I wanted more criminal law experience first, and the public defender's office is *always* hiring. What it lacks in pay, it makes up for in a heavy caseload and long hours, so the positions are hard to fill.

But even though there are only a handful of PDs and ADAs in the county, my office has been careful not to schedule me on any cases with Anderson. And I assume the

District Attorney's office has been doing the same. But nobody tells a judge no. So here I am.

"Are we going in?"

Jack's question interrupts my reverie and I realize I've come to a stop in front of the conference room door and am standing frozen, like one of the ice sculptures that will be on display in the town square all month.

"Right. Yes."

I push the door open and gesture for him to take a seat. Then I walk around to the credenza and pour each of us a glass of ice water from the pitcher sitting on a pretty red and green tray.

"You seem to know your way around here pretty well," he observes as I slide a coaster onto the table in front of him and take one for myself.

I place his glass on the coaster. "I used to work here."

"You switched sides?"

"I did. I started my career in the ADA's office right out of law school. Last summer I moved over to the public defender's office." I take a sip.

"How is it?"

I put my glass down. "The water?"

He laughs, and I try not to notice how his eyes crinkle sexily. I fail miserably. *Darn you, Delphina.*

"No. The new job."

"Oh, right." I pause and think. "I'm glad I made the move. When you're representing the government, you have this sense that you're working for the greater good. But I'm representing people. Real people. And it's different. The accused deserve representation. They deserve someone to advocate for them. To protect them. I see the system differently now that I've been on both sides of it." I feel compelled to add, "Of course, there's not much crime around here."

He's about to respond when the door swings open. Anderson stops in the doorway, his dark eyes wide, his jaw hinged open.

"Holly?" he croaks.

"Anderson," I answer coolly.

CHAPTER 6

UNLAWFUL TRESPASS

Jack

Holly's face softens as she talks about her job, and empathy peeks out from behind her brisk, business-like facade. I'm taking in the transformation, when the door swings open and a guy straight out of rich guy main casting stops, stock still, holding the door open and staring at Holly. Thick dark hair slicked back like he escaped from 1990s Wall Street, a chiseled jaw, striped prep tie, wingtips polished to a high shine—the whole deal.

After he croaks out her name and she greets him with his full first name, he blinks and clears his throat. "I'm going by Anders now."

She acts as if she hasn't heard him. "Anderson, this is my client, Jack Bell."

He squints at me for a moment then turns his attention back to her. "Anders," he repeats.

She dismisses this with a wave of her hand. "Let's work this out so we don't have to waste Judge MacIntosh's time."

"Waste his time?" he scoffs. And then, seemingly realizing he's been standing in the doorway, he steps inside, letting the door swing closed behind him. "You've got to be kidding, Holly. I've got your client dead to rights."

Her blue eyes flash. "Dead to rights doing *what*? Donating books to a little free library? You're the one who must be joking."

"Afraid not. Vicky Swanson didn't invite him onto her property. She's insisting I file criminal trespass charges and, frankly, I can see her point."

"You can see her point?" Holly's head snaps and her chin juts out. "Please, illuminate me because I can't see it."

His voice is smooth, almost soothing, when he says, "The Swansons are older. They live in a remote area without nearby neighbors. Imagine Mrs. Swanson's fear and surprise when a stranger driving a vehicle with out-of-state plates stops in her driveway and creeps through her garden under cover of darkness—"

"Come on, the sun was coming up!" I blurt.

They both turn to look at me. Holly gives her head a subtle shake.

"So the sun hadn't fully risen?" The ADA presses. "You're admitting you went there in the dark?"

"My client isn't on the record."

"Are you telling me he's lying?"

She closes her eyes and takes a breath and it reminds me of nothing so much as my second-grade teacher, Mrs. Skyler, who would visibly gather her patience before dealing with a recalcitrant boy. Sometimes that boy was me. Usually, it was me.

"Anderson," she says levelly, sounding very Mrs. Skyler-like. "The early morning, just before sunrise, is not the cover of darkness. It's civil twilight, but let's leave that aside for now. Why do the Swansons have a little free library if they don't want people to use it? Its very existence is an invitation to come onto their property."

"I don't see it that way. Neither does Vicky."

Her jaw tightens. "And what about Mr. Swanson? Does Pete support this miscarriage of justice?"

"Mr. Swanson's out of town, hauling back the Christmas tree for the town square from White Pines Farm," he informs her in a satisfied voice. "A fact that makes the intrusion even more frightening. Imagine an isolated, frightened old woman—"

"Ha! I'd like to see you call Victoria Swanson an old woman to her face."

He bobs his head at this as if she has a point but soldiers on. "A senior citizen, home alone, sees a strange man skulking around her garden before the sun's come up. You're lucky I'm not seeking stronger charges."

"Like what?" She snorts.

"Attempted burglary."

"Anderson." She pauses for a beat. "He didn't *take* any books. He added some books. Do you want to charge him with good Samaritanism? Civic responsibility? Attempted do-gooding?"

He presses his lips into a firm, thin line and flares his nostrils at her needling.

I'm no legal expert, but I don't think this is going to settle before court.

Holly must realize the same thing because she shakes her head and flips her portfolio closed with a snap. "This is a waste of my time. Let's go, Jack."

He places a hand on her arm to still her. "Holly, wait." His voice is low, a rasp.

She stares at his hand and swallows hard. After a long moment, she raises her eyes to meet his gaze with an even look. "What?"

"I wish … I mean … it's good to see you."

Her expression shutters. "Remove your hand from my arm. Now."

She sweeps past the assistant district attorney and I hurry to catch up with her.

"See you in court!" Anderson yells behind her in a transparent bid to regain the upper hand.

She snorts, maintains her pace, and doesn't turn around. When she mutters "he really frosts my cookie" under her breath, I have to bite my lip to keep from laughing.

CHAPTER 7

A COURT-ORDERED ORDEAL

Holly

I usher Jack into the courtroom and get him seated at the defense table in the otherwise-empty courtroom. Then I straighten my suit jacket, check the knot at the nape of my neck to ensure no stray tendrils of hair have escaped, and sink into the seat beside him.

"Now what happens? Jack whispers worriedly.

I manage a weak smile. "Now you have an arraignment and we get Judge MacIntosh to see the idiocy of these charges. But first, I need a minute."

I pat his arm reassuringly before I close my eyes and focus on my breathing. I need to deal with my white-hot rage at stupid Anderson and his stupid face and his stupid new name if I'm going to have any chance of making a cogent legal argument.

Breathing in, I accept my anger. Breathing out, I feel my anger. Breathing in, I hold my anger lightly. Breathing out, I release my anger.

Breathing in, my anger returns, flaring in my chest, when I hear Anderson's stupid feet clomping up toward the well. Breathing out, my eyes pop open at the sound of his stupid voice greeting the judge's courtroom deputy, who must have followed him into the room.

As Anderson settles in behind the table across the aisle, the judge's deputy crosses over to greet me.

"Hiya, Holly."

"Hi, Nate." I smile.

"Any chance you and the ADA can work this out without the judge?" He gives me a hopeful look.

"Nope. The state has taken leave of his—its—senses."

Nate huffs out a soft laugh. "I guess it was too much to expect you two to be able to play nice after all that's happened, huh?"

I bristle as I feel Jack's curious gaze on me, and I know he's wondering what Nate's talking about.

"I tried, Nate. Believe me. I tried."

Nate pats my arm, an echo of the gesture of comfort I gave my client just moments ago. Then he heads to the front of the courtroom. The door behind the bench opens, and the judge sweeps into the room, his black robe fluttering behind him and the red bells affixed to his collar jingling.

Nate intones, "All rise. The Honorable Christian MacIntosh presiding."

We pop to our feet as the judge takes his place on the bench. He peers down at us over the rims of his half-glasses.

"Be seated."

We sit.

Nate hands the judge a folder. "First up is the State of Vermont versus Jack Henry Bell. Actually, it's the only case on the arraignment docket today," he says as an aside.

I'm gratified to see the judge's eyebrows shoot up as he flips open the folder and scans the sheet. He closes the folder and gives Anderson a long look. "Do the honors, counselor."

Anderson stands and smooths his tie over his chest. "Anders Wilson Carson for the State, Your Honor. The State charges that shortly before sunrise this morning, in Mistletoe Mountain, Vermont, Jack Henry Bell knowingly entered and remained on lands of another without legal authority or the consent of the landowner, specifically by entering the property located at 128 Lake Road under cover of darkness, in violation of Title 13, Vermont Statutes Annotated, Section 3705."

Again with the cover of darkness. Then again, he *does* sleep with a nightlight.

"Do you understand the charges against you, Mr. Bell?"

I nudge him and we both stand.

"Uh, to be honest, not really."

The judge narrows his eyes then says, "I'm not asking if you agree with them. Do you know what they mean?"

"Yes," Jack says uncertainly.

Apparently satisfied, the judge turns to me. "Counsel, how does your client plead?"

"H. Evelyn Jolly for the defendant. Your Honor, Mr. Bell pleads not guilty."

He turns toward his deputy. Nate already has the calendar pulled up on his computer, ready to assign a trial date.

I clear my throat. "Your Honor, if I may?"

He gives me a nod.

"Respectfully, the State has failed to establish the elements of unlawful trespass."

At his table, Anderson clucks like a pissed-off hen. The judge and I both ignore him.

"In what way?"

"Section 3705(a) requires a no-trespassing notice, either verbal or a posted sign. As far as I know, the Swansons' property has no such signage, and the officer's affidavit doesn't mention Mrs. Swanson asking Mr. Bell to leave." I slide Anderson a *gotcha* grin.

He smirks right back at me. "While Ms. Jolly is correct about the requirements under Section 3705(a), she's mistaken that it matters."

Judge MacIntosh narrows his eyes. "How so?"

"Mr. Bell isn't charged with trespass under section a. We're charging him under section c."

I squeeze my eyes closed and try to recall the subsection of the statute. But all I can come up with is entry into a building other than a residence, and *that* can't be right. Frustrated, I shake my head and open my eyes.

Luckily, the judge is equally perplexed. He gestures for the deputy to hand him the laptop and pecks out a search one finger at a time. He studies the screen, then leans forward and reads it aloud. "The pertinent section provides, 'A person who enters a building other than a residence, whose access is normally locked, whether or not the access is actually locked, or a residence in violation of an order of any court of competent jurisdiction in this State shall be imprisoned for not more than one year or fined not more than $500.00, or both.'"

He frowns at Anderson. "There's no allegation the defendant entered a structure, locked or unlocked."

"Agreed," Anderson says entirely too cheerfully as he returns to his feet.

"Care to explain how this case fits into subsection c, counsel?"

"Happily. The structure Mr. Bell accessed was the little free library itself. While it was unlocked, Mrs. Swanson generally keeps it locked as is made clear from the placard on the box that reads 'to choose a book, ring the bell.' The bell in question is a doorbell camera that records activities at the box and sends the feed to her mobile phone."

He rocks back on his heels with a satisfied expression.

"Your Honor," I sputter, "respectfully, that is not how

little free libraries are intended to operate. Mr. Bell was entitled to rely on social norms here, placard or no placard. And again, he didn't take a book. He donated several. In light of—"

The judge holds up a hand. "Save it for trial."

"Seriously?" I blurt the word before I can catch myself.

He gives me a cautionary look. "Seriously."

I glance over at Jack, who shakes his head in disbelief. I know exactly how he feels. I pat his shoulder in a show of support.

He grabs my hand and stage whispers, "A year in prison?"

"That is *not* going to happen," I whisper back fiercely.

Nate leans over and points to the judge's calendar. The judge nods.

"Mr. Bell, your trial is set for the third of January."

Anderson and I nod in unison.

The judge asks, "What's the State's bail recommendation?"

"No bail, Your Honor."

I turn toward Anderson and tilt my head like I must've misheard him. "No bail?"

He keeps his eyes on the judge when he responds. "The defendant is not a member of this community. His driver's license, registration, and license plate indicate that he's a resident of Florida. As the court is aware, Florida is a long way from Mistletoe Mountain, Vermont. We have no confidence that he would return for trial."

I turn toward Jack. "Stand up."

He stands.

"Mr. Bell, if released on bail, will you promise to return to stand trial in the new year?"

"Of course."

He looks at me as he says this, and I jerk my head toward the bench.

He picks up the cue and addresses the court, "I will, Your Honor."

"Where do you live, Mr. Bell?" the judge asks.

"I'm a nomad," he tells the judge.

Anderson pops to his feet. "He's homeless? He's obviously a flight risk."

I grit my teeth.

"I'm not homeless, Your Honor. I'm a traveler. I go where the spirit moves me."

This has to be a nightmare. I dig my fingernails into my palms. He's going to get himself thrown back in jail.

"Where is the spirit moving you next, Mr. Bell?" the judge asks from the bench.

"I'm on my way to Montreal."

"A lovely city," the judge decrees.

Anderson leans forward like he's about to spring. "Your Honor, the defendant has just revealed his plan to flee the country."

"He doesn't want to flee the country, Anderson. He wants to go on a vacation."

"Criminals don't get to go on vacations, Holly."

"I'll have no more bickering," the judge says. "Mr. Bell, the assistant district attorney is correct. You'll have to wait until this matter's been settled to visit our neighbors to the north. Mr. Bell will turn his passport over to the court and remain in town until a hearing can be had on this matter."

"Your Honor," I try again. "My client is entitled to a speedy trial."

"This is speedy. You know this court has reduced hours during the holidays."

"Your Honor, with all due respect, Mr. Bell's constitutional rights trump holiday festivities."

The judge looks aghast at this assertion.

Beside me, Jack clears his throat. "Your Honor, I don't mind, uh, waiving my right to a fast trial or whatever. I wouldn't want to interfere with the court's plans."

"See," the judge says, as if this settles it.

I frown at my idiot client. "Surely Mr. Bell has plans of his own for the holidays. It's really not fair to keep him here. For a month. In county lock-up."

The corners of Judge MacIntosh's mouth turn down and his eyes droop thinking about Jack Bell sitting in a cell while all of Mistletoe Mountain celebrates around him.

"You're right. The court will remand him to your custody."

It takes several seconds for this statement to sink in. When it does, I go wide eyed and gasp for breath. "Sidebar, Your Honor?"

"Approach."

I turn to Jack and tell him to sit tight. Anderson uses the delay to race-walk to the bench ahead of me.

As soon as I catch up, I maneuver in front of him and whisper, "Your Honor, I live in a one-bedroom apartment. It would hardly be appropriate."

The judge scoffs, "I'm remanding him to your custody, not to your loft."

"I don't understand, Your Honor."

"Take him to the inn." As I'm processing this idea, he adds, "You'll also have to stay there, of course."

"Your Honor, this is very unusual, and I—"

"I was under the impression you don't have plans for the holiday, Holly." A faint smile crosses his lips.

It's at this moment that I realize Christian MacIntosh, my sister Ivy's godfather, a distant relative on my mom's side, has been talking to my father. Or my father's fiancée. Someone has shared my plan to hole up with my pile of books this holiday season.

"Uncle Chris, Please don't do this. I don't want to be at the inn for Christmas."

"Is that your legal argument, Holly?"

"No, I'm throwing myself at the mercy of the court," I counter.

"The inn is so festive this time of year," he responds mercilessly.

Anderson just stands there with a stupid grin pasted on his stupid face.

"Does the state have a position on my order?" the judge asks.

"Your Honor, I think the county lock-up is sufficient," Anderson says.

"The Court disagrees. You withdraw the no-bail argument or I remand the defendant into Ms. Jolly's custody until trial."

Anderson's sugarplum-eating grin vanishes. If he agrees to bail, he'll have to go back to the office and admit I outmaneuvered him. If he doesn't, I'll have to spend the month of December babysitting a hot, albeit scruffy, book lover in a winter wonderland of hell. I silently implore him with my eyes, but I already know what he'll choose. He's chosen it before. He picked his career over my happiness when we were a couple. Of course, he'll do it now. And he does.

"Upon reflection, the state agrees with Your Honor's order," Anderson says.

I can't pretend to be surprised. Looking at him now, it's hard to believe I ever found his raw ambition attractive.

"Step back." The judge shoos us away from the bench. Once we're back at our respective tables, I give Jack a reassuring smile even though I feel slightly queasy.

"Is there anything else?" The judge's tone makes clear the only correct answer is no.

"Yes, Your Honor," Anderson says.

Of course there is.

He ignores my loud sigh and continues, "The district

attorney's office would like the court to order the contraband in the defendant's car to be seized as evidence."

"Contraband?" I whisper-hiss at my client. "Are there drugs in your car?"

"What?" He gives me a bewildered look. "No!"

"What contraband?" I demand.

"The books."

"The books?" The judge and I both echo.

"May I approach?" Anderson asks.

The judge waves him forward. He hands me an inventory and a photograph and takes a copy of each up to the court. I study the photo. The tailgate of a red station wagon is raised, revealing two rows of boxes tidily packed full of books.

"Your Honor, even if Mr. Bell is ultimately found guilty of trespassing, which I am sure he won't be, the books themselves are not contraband or illegal in any way."

"They're evidence of his criminal enterprise," Anderson argues.

"Will you be serious for a minute, Anderson?" I snap, out of patience.

"The district attorney's point, while strained, is not completely off the mark, Ms. Jolly."

I take one look at Jack's stricken expression and dig in my heels. I am *not* letting Anderson take these books. This is a hill I'll die on.

"Noelle Winters," I blurt.

"What about her?" The judge's tone is curious.

"She can take possession of the books until Mr. Bell wins his trial." I turn to Jack. "Noelle runs the Mistletoe Mountain Library. She's a friend—and she's engaged to my father. She'll hold on to these for you." I turn back to the judge. "If that's satisfactory to the Court, of course."

"It is. Now then, there's a maple-glazed donut with my name on it," the judge says. He gives us a nod and rises from the bench, his bells jangling. "Hope to see you all at the tree lighting," he calls over his shoulder.

CHAPTER 8

NO ROOM AT THE INN

Jack

As Holly predicted, the librarian is thrilled to take the books off my hands. "Oh, these are fabulous," she murmurs as she runs a reverent finger along a row of spines.

"They're a loan, Noelle," Holly reminds her.

"Yeah, yeah," she waves her off, then beams at me. "I'll take good care of them for you."

"I appreciate it. If you're missing any of these in your collection, you can feel free to keep them. I have multiple copies of all of these, as you can see." I spread my hands over the assorted boxes like a game show host.

Noelle looks up from the cargo hold with a quizzical smile.

"What?" Holly asks.

"I didn't think there was a theme here. But there is, isn't there?"

I nod. "There is."

Holly purses her lips and studies the titles, murmuring more to herself than to us. "Different genres, different time periods, different locations." She shakes her head. "Somebody want to fill me in?"

"They're all on the banned books list," Noelle tells her.

She gasps—actually gasps—and her hands fly up to cover her heart. "These books are banned?"

"Some places," Noelle clarifies. "It would be more accurate to say they've all been challenged."

"But why?" Holly's voice is edged with disbelief.

I give her a skeptical look. "Have you been living in a cave? It's a thing. It's happening all over the country."

"Not here," She insists.

Noelle smiles ruefully. "Well, not yet."

Holly wheels around. "You expect it to?"

"It's coming. The library's gotten a flurry of complaints."

"People are *complaining* about books?"

The librarian nods. "To be fair, one person's complaining, but she's complaining enough for the whole town." She pauses. "Vicky Swanson."

Holly groans. "Of course it's her."

"So far, she's settled for notes through the mail slot or under my office door. I removed the suggestion box a long time ago thanks to her. When I get one of her love notes, I write one of my own thanking her for her interest in our collection and attach a donation form to it. Unless and until she goes to the county council, I'm not giving her any of my energy."

"If she organizes a campaign, you'll be in the same shape as a lot of other towns. Books are being taken off the shelves at schools, libraries, even some bookstores," I tell them.

Holly eases a copy of *The Outsiders* out of one of the boxes and caresses the cover. When she speaks, her voice is soft.

"My sisters and I loved this book. Must've read it a dozen times each. Why is *it* banned?"

I tick reasons off on my fingers. "Pick your reason—profanity, violence, drinking and smoking. But a favorite is family dysfunction. That and glamorizing gang life."

She snorts and returns the book to its slot. "Unreal. That's why you put these books in little free libraries—because they've been banned?"

"Yep."

"So how'd you end up here? We don't have book bans." She casts a glance at Noelle. "Yet."

"I'm passing through. I don't *only* put them in little free libraries where they're banned from the public systems. Everybody needs books, right?"

"Everybody except Mrs. Swanson."

"Yeah, I guess I picked the wrong house."

"You think?" Holly cracks.

Noelle turns away. "I'll get Farah and some volunteers to help us bring these inside."

"Wait." Holly touches the sleeve of the librarian's fuzzy cardigan sweater. "I need another favor."

Noelle's green eyes twinkle behind her glasses. "Anything for you, Holly."

"I know I said I wasn't going to stay at the inn this year, but … plans have changed. I assume all the guest rooms are booked?"

Noelle chortles, "Yeah. They have been since March."

"I figured as much. I'll ask Ivy or Merry to double up with me so Jack has a place to stay."

"Honey, I have bad news. There's no room at the inn."

"No, I mean the family wing," she clarifies.

"Oh!" Noelle catches her breath. "I guess your dad hasn't told you yet."

"Told me what?"

"Remember that big snowfall last week, right before the weekend?"

"What about it?"

"The roof over the family wing gave way. It collapsed. Our bedroom and bathroom were unscathed but the rest of the rooms aren't habitable. Renata's Repairs put a temporary tarp up until Renata can get a new roof installed. But it won't be until after the new year."

Holly stammers, "But how are we going to help with the Christmas activities?"

"Merry and Ivy are going to stay at their place and

commute back and forth, like you'd planned to from the loft. Can't you find room for Jack at your place?"

Holly casts a glance at me before answering.

"Come on, you've seen it. It's a one-bedroom open loft. It's barely big enough for me. Besides, the judge specifically said we were to stay at the inn and that's what the district attorney agreed to. There's a court order."

"Why does the district attorney care if you …?" Noelle trails off and groans. "Tell me Anderson's not on the other side."

Holly wrinkles her nose. "The one and only."

"Gah." Noelle shakes her head.

I attempt to lighten the mood. "Does your family have a manger?"

Noelle giggles, but Holly lets out an exasperated whoosh of air.

"It's not funny. You'll wish you were staying in a manger, Jack. If I can't figure out how to comply with Judge MacIntosh's order, you'll be back in county lockup until next year."

I feel the color drain from my face as my skin goes cold. The gray hours I spent in the county lock-up this morning rush back. Thirty days of that? I don't want to imagine it.

"We won't let that happen," Noelle says in a hurry. "We'll come up with something."

Despite the conviction in the librarian's voice, Holly looks unconvinced. Her fingers drum against the spine of *The Outsiders*, still clutched in her right hand.

"Like what?" she demands.

"Like, for instance, your dad and I could stay at the fishing cabin and commute back and forth. You and Jack can take our room. I'll roll in a cot—"

"You can't. No way." Holly's voice cracks slightly before she steadies it. "Dad has to be on the property full-time during the busiest time of year." I recognize that tone—it's the same one she used in court when she realized my case was going to trial. She's looking for the best way out of a bad situation.

Noelle eases the slim book out of Holly's hand. "Leave the books. Go talk to your dad. If anyone can work a miracle, it's Nick."

Holly smiles faintly. "Well, that's the truth."

I toss Noelle the keys to my car and trail Holly to her sedan, parked at the far end of the parking lot. My boots crunch through the packed snow and the sound echoes like a cell door slamming. I sure hope they're right about Nick Jolly's miracle worker abilities—because right now, he's all that stands between me and a month-long stay in a jail cell. Talk about a blue Christmas.

CHAPTER 9

ONLY ONE BED

Holly

Jack folds himself into my car and racks the passenger seat way back. He's tall, but not *that* tall. Then I remember how I pushed the seat all the way up to load the back seat as full as possible with the last of my belongings from my old place—the one I shared with Anderson. What Delphina, my sisters, and I couldn't shove into the car, I simply abandoned. Giving up my stuff was a small price to pay to not have to see Anderson again. I laugh bitterly at the thought.

Jack cuts his eyes toward me, curious. I pretend not to notice and flip on the radio. Unsurprisingly, the local station is playing Christmas music.

He hums along to "Santa Baby" for a moment before I snap off the radio. It's not even officially December and

I've had my fill of Christmas songs. Fa-la-la-la-la-la-just-my-luck.

He clears his throat in the sudden silence. "Noelle seems great."

"She is."

Noelle's *so* great. She'll never replace my mom, but then, she isn't trying to. She and my dad are happy, genuinely happy. And I'm genuinely happy for them, even though I'm convinced happily ever after is a straight-up scam.

We lapse back into silence. Then, as I'm pulling into the alley behind the inn, I ask the question that's been on my mind since the arraignment. "You really don't have plans with your family for Christmas?"

"I really don't."

I wait, but he doesn't elaborate.

Even though I park in the back, I want Jack to get the full experience of walking into the Inn at Mistletoe Mountain, so we follow the cobblestone path to the walkway around the house to the front. As we pass by the family wing, I glance up at the roof and stifle a giggle. Renata's temporary tarp is camouflaged by a dusting of glittering, decorative fake snow. Leave it to my dad to make lemonade out of that lemon.

As we round the house, I pause before mounting the steps to the wide front porch. Seeing my childhood home all dressed up for the holidays floods me with warmth, nostalgia, and longing even now, in my anti-Christmas era.

When we were girls, Ivy proclaimed that the sight made her feel like she swallowed the sun, and, now, in this moment, I finally know what she meant.

Snow sparkles on the lawn and garlands of greens intertwined with tiny white lights wind around the railings and drape the porch's roof. I crane my neck to take in the simple wreaths that grace all eight front windows, each one hanging from a wide, red ribbon, before leading Jack up the stairs. Two life-sized nutcracker soldier statues flank the entrance, as if they're standing guard. Two large, vibrant wreaths hang on the double doors. Ivy and my dad make these floral wreaths every year. This year's wreaths might be the best yet. They've used red velvet celosia, strawberry globe amaranth, and bright red salal berries.

"Wow," Jack breathes out as he takes it all in.

Despite my current anti-Christmas stance, I have to grin. "You haven't seen anything yet."

I open the door and we step inside.

The lobby is awash with twinkling lights, fragrant greens, and the distinctive spicy, citrus scent of pomander balls that hang from the wall sconces. Nutcrackers of every imaginable persuasion—traditional, fantastical, whimsical—are displayed on the built-in bookcases. Soft instrumental music plays, a welcome respite from the version of "Rocking Around the Christmas Tree" that's stuck in my head. All that's missing is the giant concolor fir we'll put up this weekend, per tradition, and invite our guests to help decorate throughout the month.

Before I can pilot Jack through the lobby, my dad swoops in from the back of the house with a hearty, "Ho, ho, hello!"

"Dad, Jack Bell. Jack, Nick Jolly, the proprietor of the Inn at Mistletoe Mountain and my dad."

"Welcome, welcome. Come on in." Dad lunges forward to give Jack an enthusiastic handshake, gripping his elbow with his left hand as he pumps Jack's hand with his right. Noelle jokes that my dad has real golden retriever energy. She's not wrong.

"Mr. Jolly, it's a pleasure—" Jack begins.

"Call me Nick," Dad instructs before turning to sweep me into a quick, tight hug. "Hi, Holls." He releases me and holds me at arm's length, studying me with a wry smile. "I hear your Uncle Chris gave you the business in court."

Humiliating news travels fast—an immutable fact of small-town life.

I groan. "I'm guessing Noelle called."

"She did, and I have a solution."

Bless this man. "Already? What is it?"

"Wait—the judge is your uncle?" Jack wades into the conversation, no doubt appalled by the impropriety.

"Not really," my dad assures him. "Chris is my late wife's second cousin. But he's our middle daughter's godfather, so the girls have always called him Uncle Chris."

Jack nods, either clear on the matter or pretending that he gets it.

I bring the conversation back to a more pressing topic. "What's your plan, Dad?"

"The guest cottage just became available."

That's impossible, I think.

"How? The Bryants reserve it every year."

"They do," he agrees. "But Jodi and Mark's kids all pitched in to surprise them with a two-week cruise for their fiftieth anniversary. The whole family's going. I'll spare you all the details, but after a twenty-five-minute-long logistical phone call with Mark this morning, it became clear that getting from Tennessee to here and then to Los Angeles, where the cruise starts, wasn't feasible. I think he was on the verge of tears. So I refunded his deposit, rebooked him for next December, and wished him a *bon voyage.* Long story short, Noelle called before I had a chance to start working my way down the waitlist. It's yours if you want it."

Relief floods my body. Problem solved. Then I freeze. "Wait."

"There's only one bed." My father is *smirking.* Like this is funny. It's very not funny.

Jack clears his throat. "I think I have a sleeping bag in my car. I can bunk on the floor."

See? Tent camper. And apparently a gentleman, which makes this whole situation even more awkward somehow.

This declaration wipes the smirk right off my dad's face. It's replaced by a look of horror. "Absolutely not."

"Really, it's no problem," Jack assures him.

Dad shakes his head. "Nonsense. You're a guest."

I raise both hands. "You know what? It's fine. I'll sleep on the couch."

This appeases my father even though he and I both know I'm too tall to stretch out on the couch—more of a loveseat, really—that he and Noelle put in at the end of the summer so they could give the old leather couch to a family who lost everything in a fire. But, it's only for a month. I'll survive.

Jack's frowning like he's going to argue, but I cut him off. "Save your breath. Nick Jolly is nothing if not focused on the comfort and delight of every guest."

"I'm not really a guest," he counters, no doubt acutely aware that this situation is beyond weird.

"Every guest," I repeat. "Even the ones foisted on him by order of court." As soon as I say *foisted,* I regret it.

My dad glares at me before saying, "You haven't been foisted on me, Jack. We're delighted to have you."

He reaches over the gleaming walnut registration desk and lifts a red hiking backpack from the shelf under the desk. It's stuffed full and obviously well loved. It was also confiscated by the police, and I had drafting a motion to get it back on my list for this afternoon.

"How?" I ask, even though I should know better than to question my dad's magical ability to make things easier.

"I ran into Officer Liza at the post office. She'd just heard about the judge's order, so she offered to bring it by after she mailed her package."

Offered. Right. Dollars to apple cider donuts, he promised to save her and her wife spots in Ivy's wreath-making workshop. Mrs. Officer Liza is a crafter, and Ivy's workshops fill up fast. The county police, like almost everyone who works at the court complex, mainly live in the valley, not here in town. And while they love to joke about how corny Mistletoe Mountain is, come December, they're suddenly big fans.

"However you got it, thanks. You've freed up a couple hours of my time."

He claps his hands together. "Perfect! Then you have no excuse not to join us for dinner and the tree lighting."

I suppress a groan and hedge. "We'll see."

CHAPTER 10

SWEET TREATS AND A BITTER PHONE CALL

Jack

Holly shows me around the guest cottage with the nervous energy of a big cat— a panther or maybe a jaguar.

"Here's the kitchen," she says, as if the appliances and cabinets didn't give it away.

"Living room," she gestures to the room anchored by a sofa that looks too short for her to sleep on. We'll have to revisit this plan.

She continues, pacing through the room. "There's a beautiful view of the mountains from the chair by the window." Her tone is as clipped as her steps.

She waves an arm toward a closed door. "Bedroom and shower."

"Great," I say. "Perfect. But forget what your dad said. You take the bed."

"No, really, it's my job."

I shake my head. "I'm pretty sure housing clients isn't a lawyer's responsibility."

She laughs, "True. Except that, in this case, it was either put you up or leave you in jail. And I do have a duty not to let you cool your heels in county lockup for a month."

A month. I still can't believe I'm stuck here for a month.

"But beyond that," she continues, "I'm the daughter of an innkeeper. I was raised from the time I could crawl to extend hospitality to guests. It's in my DNA. And there's no way I'm letting you sleep on the couch."

"And I'm not taking the only bed," I insist.

We lock eyes.

She breaks the standoff with a sigh. "We'll fight about it later. I need to go into the office for a few hours and prepare a client file for you."

I look around the cottage, decorated within an inch of its life to look like a sweet gingerbread house. "Do I have to stay here or am I allowed to walk around town without you as an escort?"

She catches her full lower lip between her teeth. "Good question. The order doesn't say you're under house arrest, but I should ask the judge to clarify the terms. I'll call his chambers on my way to my office."

"I didn't mean to add more work to your plate."

"Listen. This part is my job. Don't worry about it." She

grabs her keys from the counter and heads toward the door. "I'll be back in two or three hours, max. For now, just hang out. Watch a movie or read a book. There's food in the fridge. Or you could take a hot shower and wash the jail off of you."

This last idea holds some appeal.

"I'll be fine," I assure her.

She leaves and I watch from the window over the sink as she pulls out of her parking spot. Then I rummage through my backpack for my cell phone to make a call I know I need to make but definitely don't want to.

I groan, run my hands through my hair, and drop the phone on the counter. I'll shower first. Then make the call.

Before I've taken two steps toward the bedroom, there's a knock at the door. Is Holly back already? I look through the window to see a curvy woman with a mess of dark curly hair and a wide grin standing on the porch. Her arms are full.

I open the door.

"Hi," she chirps. "I'm Merry, the youngest Jolly daughter. And you must be Jack."

"I am, in fact. Come on in."

"I'd shake your hand, but—," she gestures with her arms, which are full of tumblers and white pastry bags. "Sweet Merry's" is stamped on the sides of the bags under a drawing of a food truck decorated for the holidays.

I hold out my hands to take some of the items and she

gestures toward the tumblers with her chin. "You could grab the coffees."

I do as directed. She follows me in and kicks the door closed behind her. Then she dumps the bags on the kitchen island and starts pawing through them while I stand there holding the tumblers.

She procures a silver platter from a drawer set in the island and starts arranging the goodies on it. "The pink travel mug is yours. Apparently Officer Ned returned it to Delphina after …" she trails off.

"He arrested me on the sidewalk." I finish for her.

She shakes her head. "Sorry about him. Ned's a bit intense. Anyway, Delphina made you a fresh drink. It's still hot. And whatever it is, it smells *amazing.*"

"Gingerbread latte with candy cane foam."

Her eyes widen. "Yum, great choice. That one's heavenly—I call it dessert in a mug."

Her enthusiasm is infectious.

"I only had a sip, but that sounds right."

"Drink up!" she insists.

I set the light blue tumbler on the island. "Is this one yours?"

"No, it's a peace offering for Holly."

I take a long swallow of my sweet concoction as she goes on with a snort.

"Black coffee. Nothing but the unadulterated bean, as Holly would say." She shakes her head. "Just between us,

I'm not even sure my sister likes desserts, but she at least pretends to for my sake."

"Oh, come on. Everybody likes dessert." To prove the point, I grab a cookie dotted with dried cherries and dark chocolate chunks and polish it off with two big bites. "Mmmm."

Her already broad grin widens even further. "I like you, Jack Bell. By the way, where *is* Holly? I didn't see her car."

"She headed into her office for a few hours."

"Of course she did. Well, please let her know that dinner's going to be early tonight. We're eating at five and then heading to the Christmas tree lighting."

"I don't think your sister wants to go," I inform her gravely.

She waves a hand. "She'll come around. Despite what she thinks, locking herself away with a pile of books and pretending it's not the holidays isn't going to help her get over it any faster."

"Get over what?"

She opens her mouth, reconsiders, then clamps it shut dramatically. "Nothing. Pretend I didn't say anything."

"You didn't," I point out.

Her face softens. "It's not my story to tell. Let's just say, Holly isn't really feeling the holiday spirit this year."

"I get that much. I'm wondering why."

She evades the question, bubbly as ever. "I need to get back. Enjoy your 'pressert,' and I'll see you at dinner."

She flits out the door and heads down the path. I half

expect to see bluebirds alighting on her shoulders as she traipses toward the back to the inn.

I remove the lid from my Snowflake Cafe travel tumbler and inhale the sweet spicy aroma of the drink. I take another gulp before I select a chocolate marshmallow brownie from the array Merry left, sinking my teeth into the gooey goodness.

After fortifying myself with caffeine and sugar, I'm ready to get it over with. I pick up my phone, open my contacts, and am faced with a choice: I can call Roger or Sam. Who better to break this news to? My evil stepfather or my disapproving brother? When I put it like that, it's a no-brainer.

I jab Sam's contact icon.

He picks up on the fourth ring, right before the call rolls to voicemail. "Where the devil are you, Jack?"

"Hello to you, too, Sam. I'm in Mistletoe Mountain, Vermont."

"Vermont? I haven't heard from you since … Maryland?"

"Right. Maryland. I called your office a couple times, but Janey said you were in London, and with the time difference …"

"Yeah, just got back. Still adjusting."

"What's in London?" I sit on the couch, lean back, and stretch my legs out in front of me.

"That producer who reached out a few months ago. He's on location, and I flew there to see if we could hammer out a deal face-to-face."

"And?"

"And he wants to see how the trust shakes out."

The flatness in his voice is a reminder that what he really means is the producer wants to see how *I* shake out. We sit in silence for a few seconds, then Sam relents.

"So how's Mistletoe Mountain? Sounds like something straight out of a Hallmark movie."

I chuckle. "From what I've seen it is. Loads of holiday cheer, but I did run into a wrinkle."

My brother sighs. "Did you let your passport expire? I guess you aren't going to Canada."

"Nope, I renewed it before I started the trip."

"Out of money?" he guesses again.

Almost, I think.

"No." I clear my throat. "There was ... a misunderstanding with the local authorities."

"Did you wreck? Were you speeding?"

"Stop guessing. You're not going to guess it."

"You robbed a bank."

"What?!"

"You said I wouldn't be able to guess. Just thinking outside the box."

"I put a couple books in a little free library."

"I would hope so. That's why you're on this boondoggle. So?"

"So, apparently the owner of this little free library doesn't like people giving or taking books without a formal invitation."

Sam falls silent. Then, he says. "Is that not the point of a little free library?"

"It is," I confirm. "Try telling that to Mrs. Vicky Swanson. She called the cops. I've been charged with unlawful trespass."

He guffaws. "That's hilarious, bro."

"Yeah, it would be. If the DA wasn't taking it seriously."

"So what, you have to pay a fine? I'll wire you the cash. The story'll be worth however much it costs."

"You don't get it, Sam. I had an arraignment this morning. My lawyer got me out, but I had to surrender my passport. And I have to stay in town until the first week of January for my trial. If I'm found guilty, I could face up to a year in prison."

All the mirth is gone from his voice. "A year in prison for donating books?"

"It's unbelievable, right?"

He's not listening.

"Roger's gonna hit the ceiling."

"That's why we're not going to tell him," I say.

"And how's that going to work? How am I supposed to explain a month-long absence over the holidays? You're supposed to fly back from Montreal, remember?"

"Yeah, I remember. But, luckily, since the irresponsible, ne'er-do-well shoe fits me so well, just tell him I met a girl. He'll believe that."

"That could work," Sam muses. Then his voice sharpens with suspicion. "*Did* you meet a girl?"

"No," I protest. "Well, yes. But no."

"Yes, but no? You know what, never mind. We need to get you a lawyer."

"I told you, I have one. The girl is a public defender."

"Jack, if you're really facing potential jail time, you need a *good* lawyer. I'll make some calls."

Sam is such a snob. I feel compelled to defend Holly. "Believe me, she's good, and she knows how to push the DA's buttons. There's some kind of history there."

"A history? That's not good."

"I think it's more upsetting to him than her. I don't know the whole story yet, but since the judge said my choices were to spend the month in county lockup or have her take custody of me, I'll have plenty of time to ask."

"Wait, you're staying with this woman?"

"I know, it's ludicrous. But, her family owns an inn and—"

"Oh, so you're staying at the inn."

"Well, the inn's booked."

"Staying in the manger?"

"Heh, I made that joke, too. She didn't think it was funny."

"A lawyer without a sense of humor. Go figure. So if the inn is booked and you're not staying at her place, where *are* you staying?"

"There's a guest cottage behind the inn. The judge said it would be inappropriate for me to stay at Holly's apartment, but apparently, it's completely appropriate for the two of us to stay in this cottage. I guess because the Jollys are such upstanding members of the community or something."

"The Jollys?"

"Her family."

"Wait, wait. Your lawyer's name is Holly Jolly?"

I listen as Sam roars with laughter for at least a solid minute.

He starts to talk again, then stops himself. "I can't breathe. Hang on."

After a moment, I ask, "Have you pulled yourself together yet?"

I can almost see him wiping the tears of laughter from his eyes, sitting at his polished desk in his three-piece suit, despite the fact that I've explained multiple times that nobody under the age of fifty wears a vest.

"I'm good now. Whew, Holly Jolly. You're the best, Jack. Also the worst."

"Thanks," I say dryly. "So can you run interference with Roger or what?"

"Yeah—and the board. Luckily I have plenty of practice cleaning up your messes."

"You're welcome," I deadpan.

He snorts.

"Seriously, though. Thanks, Sam."

"Don't mention it. You've got to stay out of trouble, though."

"I *have* been staying out of trouble."

"And yet, you managed to get yourself arrested."

"Bite me. This isn't my fault."

His voice turns serious. "Whether it's your fault or not, if this hits the national press, it's going to be a disaster. Especially after your stunt at the funeral."

I tamp down the urge to shoot back. There's no point in rehashing the same argument for the billionth time.

"I know," I say in an effort to stave off the rest of the lecture. It doesn't work.

"Your heart's in the right place, Jack, but sometimes your brain—"

"Gotta run," I say brusquely, ending the call before he can reprise the refrain I've been hearing my entire life.

Jack, the flaky good-hearted one. Jack, the one who stumbles into trouble like a bumbling fool. Jack, the irresponsible, good-time guy. Jack, the impulsive one who acts before he thinks.

This road trip is supposed to show that I can be responsible, that I have substance, and that I can be trusted with important things. And, somehow, I've mucked it up. Story of my life.

CHAPTER 11

THE NEGOTIATION

Holly

I race into the cottage, chased by the cold, stamping my feet and pushing my windblown hair out of my face. I drop my coat on a chair and the bag I grabbed from my loft on the floor beside it before I realize Jack's asleep on the couch. I freeze, instantly regretting my loud entrance.

He stirs but doesn't wake. I slip off my shoes and creep silently across the floor. I spot the platter piled high with treats on the kitchen island and recognize Merry's handiwork. There's a Snowflake Cafe tumbler upside down in the sink and another, right side up, on the island. I lift the lid from the one on the island, peer inside, and smile as I inhale steam and the unmistakable scent of coffee, just plain old coffee. I take a long drink of the still-hot brew and recognize it as the Stonebridge Roasters' Arabica blend that Delphina stocks especially for me. She's officially forgiven.

I savor the coffee, then break off a corner from a piece of Merry's addictively good toffee and nibble it while I study the man dozing on the couch. His tanned face is relaxed in repose and his unfairly long eyelashes brush his cheeks. Sleeping, he seems younger. This observation makes me realize I don't know how old he is. The sum total of what I know about Jack Bell is that he drives a red station wagon, must like books, and is either independently wealthy or broke and unemployed. Taking in his broken-in boots, faded jeans, and scruffy beard, I'm betting on the latter. I can't think about it too much or the fact that I'm essentially living with a stranger for the next month will freak me out.

He jolts awake and I hurry to avert my eyes from his face to the array of goodies on the tray. I catch him scrubbing his hand over his eyes and chin, and look up.

"Nice nap?" I ask.

He gives me a groggy look, and I see in his eyes the moment he remembers where he is, and why. He clears his throat and sits up straighter. "How long have you been back?"

"Maybe a minute. I think I woke you up when I came in." I lie because the alternative is to tell him, oh, just long enough to watch you sleep while I drank my coffee, which would probably freak him out about staying with me.

He narrows his eyes and gives me a close look. I smile innocently and pop a chocolate peppermint in my mouth. He holds my gaze a moment longer and it's like looking in a funhouse mirror, well minus the tan and scruffy beard— his eyes are the exact shade of cornflower blue as mine. I refuse to look away first.

He blinks and I hide a smile. Amateur.

He gestures toward the desserts. "Your sister said to tell you dinner is at five. And then we're all going to the tree lighting."

I pick up my coffee, walk into the living room, and pull the armchair close to the couch. Once I'm seated, I lean forward and search his face. "We need to talk."

One eyebrow crawls up his forehead. "Sounds serious."

"It is." I reach into my bag and remove the revised order. "Judge MacIntosh clarified his order. You don't have to spend every minute with me. The judge realizes I have a job, and there's no point in making you stay in this cottage. If he did that, you might as well just be in prison. But you have a curfew. Once the streetlights come on, you can't be outside without me."

"What am I, twelve?" he cracks, but the bobbing of his throat gives away his bravado.

"No, Jack. You're a criminal defendant. So, between dusk and dawn, you need to be with me." This comes out wrong, and I feel my cheeks heat. I hurry past it. "The judge also recommended, but didn't order, that you attend some of the holiday festivities while you're in town. Don't worry, we don't have to go to all of them."

"That's no problem. I love Christmas. I want to go to as many as I can."

Judging by the way the corner of his lip quirks up, he's being sincere. I groan inwardly. Just my luck.

"Whoa, slow down. There's a stipulation."

"Okay, hit me."

I twitch my mouth to the side. "I have to attend them with you."

"The ones at night?"

"No, all of them. Which, for the record, will not be all of them."

"Why not?"

"Where to start?" I tick reasons off on my fingers. "One, I have a job to do. A job that includes keeping you out of prison. Two, this town has approximately six billion winter activities between tonight and New Year's Day. It's not even physically possible to attend them all. And you'd have to be a masochist to want to. Which leads me to the third reason. I don't want to. And since you can't go unless I go, you're not going to them all."

His mouth turns down and he thinks for a minute. "But you said the judge wants me to."

I sigh. "He thinks it would be good for the community to get to know you as something other than a criminal. If Anderson doesn't drop this and it goes to trial, we'll seat a jury from Mistletoe Mountain because the Swansons technically live within the town limits. So the holiday events are a chance for you to show people who you are."

He grins. "People love me."

His smile is so open and genuine that I can see why, but I maintain a neutral expression. "Let's hope so."

Aside from the fact that it's a solid defense strategy, I have reasons of my own for following the judge's advice. The main one being, he's the chief judge for the county and I'm going to appear before him dozens more times. I don't want to tick him off. That said, there's a limit to how many Christmas activities I'm willing to do.

I set the order aside and hand Jack the full-color Mistletoe Mountain Merriment Calendar that I grabbed from the stack in the lobby of my apartment building.

He scans it, grin widening. "This is awesome. Look at these—there's a 5k run, a snowman-building contest, ice skating, a concert in the park … there's something every day."

"I know. Pick two for each week."

His head jerks up. "Two? I can't pick just two. How about four?"

"Four a week? Absolutely not."

He exhales. "Okay, three."

"No way, Jack."

He holds my gaze and drops his voice into a low, husky whisper. "Please? This might be old hat to you, but we don't all live in a winter wonderland. This is my chance to make up for all those Christmases at the beach in Florida."

I'm about to play the world's smallest violin for him, but something in his soft voice stops me. I sit back in my chair. "You really never had a white Christmas?"

"No." Then he pauses. "Okay, that isn't true. We did spend one Christmas with my dad's folks in Colorado before he split. I'm told it snowed there, but I was three. I don't remember it."

"Your dad left your mom?"

He nods. "He wanted to 'find himself.'"

The air quotes tell me I probably know the answer, but I still ask. "Did he?"

"I guess so. He found himself at the bottom of the ocean when the catamaran he was sailing around the world sank in the Torres Strait."

His voice is cool, but pain flickers in his clear blue eyes.

"I'm sorry, Jack."

He tries to shrug it off, but I reach over and squeeze his hand. "I lost my mom a year and a half ago. It still hits me in waves."

He covers my hand with his free one. "Thanks. And I'm sorry. My mom passed away recently, too. I know what you mean. But believe me, that's not what I feel about my father."

"It sure looks like grief," I venture.

He takes a moment to answer. "If I grieve anything it's the choices he made when he was alive, not his death."

I consider this, then clear my throat. "Got it."

He brightens. "So does my status as an orphan melt your icy heart enough to agree to four events a week?"

Despite myself, I laugh at the dark humor. "Let's meet in the middle. I'll agree to three. That gives you one dozen holiday activities."

He sighs. "Fine, three. I don't understand what you have against jumping in wholeheartedly."

A lot, I think. The last time I jumped into something wholeheartedly, I made an absolute fool of myself. But I'm not about to say any of this to him.

"I don't have anything against the celebrations. I've lived here a long time, though. So I'm kind of over them."

It's a weak reason, and I can tell he doesn't believe it. In a bid to change the subject, I glance pointedly at the clock hanging over the mantle. His gaze follows mine.

"I didn't realize how late it was. I still need to hit the shower before dinner."

He stands and stretches his arms overhead, and I pretend not to see the flash of flat abdominal muscle when his argyle sweater lifts. I turn away fast, my cheeks burning, and busy myself in the kitchen until he starts to pad toward the bedroom.

"There should be towels and toiletries set up because the house was already made up for the Bryants. But if there's anything you need that you can't find, give a shout."

He nods, then pads across the room and disappears into the bedroom. After a moment, I hear the shower turn on.

Maybe this won't be so bad, I encourage myself. It's only a month, after all. We'll be smack in the heart of the festivities because the inn is Christmas Central this time of year.

Of course, this prime location is exactly why I planned to avoid the inn. But, on the bright side, the cottage is super cute and I can still plow through my pile of books on the four nights a week that I *don't* have to fake Christmas cheer. Besides, maybe it's better to face the town and my failure head-on rather than prolonging the pain by avoiding everyone until the new year.

Rip the band-aid off, I tell myself as I stack the plethora of treats into a glass storage container. Lost in thought, I don't register the sound of the water turning off. So when Jack materializes in the doorway from the bedroom wearing a candy cane-striped towel slung low around his hips, a sheepish grin, and absolutely nothing else, my grip on the platter slips. I lunge for it and barely manage to catch it before it falls to the floor.

"Forgot my bag." He dashes across the living room, grabs his backpack, and disappears behind the door.

I place the platter down carefully, press my palms against the kitchen counter, and look out the window over the sink, focusing on the sound of my shaky breath and the sight of the icy gray-blue sky until the image of the mostly naked man in the next room fades from my mind.

The door opens again a few minutes later and Jack emerges fully dressed, his thick blonde hair damp from the shower. In place of the sweater and faded jeans, he wears khaki pants and a forest green long-sleeved shirt.

"Sorry about that."

I wave it off as though it's no big deal. "Don't worry about it. I need to get ready, too."

I scoop up my bag and dart into the master bedroom, trading my severe work suit for a wine-colored, knee-length sweater dress and low-heeled black boots. I run a brush through my hair and pile it on top of my head in a loose knot. Then I swipe a lipstick in a shade that matches the dress over my lips and stick it in my pocket for later touch-ups. A minute later, I join Jack in the living room.

His gaze travels slowly over my body, then lands on my face, where it lingers. "You look festive," he rasps.

A tingle works its way up my spine. "Thanks." We lock eyes for a beat too long. I swallow. "We should go."

He hands me my coat from the chair and I shrug into it while he puts on his jacket.

"I was thinking," he says, as I lock the door and we start down the walkway from the guesthouse to the main house. The sun still hangs low in the sky but our path is already lit by the glow of tiny white twinkle lights strung overhead and big red globe lights nestled in the trees.

"About what?"

"I don't think the Christmas tree lighting should count as one of my twelve events."

"On what basis?"

"I didn't ask to go. Your dad and sister basically insisted. In fact, everyone we've seen in town has said, 'Will I see you at the tree lighting?' or 'See you at the tree lighting.' So this one seems mandatory."

He makes a pretty good argument, especially for a layperson. But like any halfway decent lawyer, I turn it around on him.

"Precisely because the whole town will be there, you really need to attend. It's a high-value opportunity, not a freebie."

"Don't think of it as a freebie. Think of it as a bonus. Like a baker's dozen."

"Nice try. I'm a lawyer, not a baker."

Undaunted, he tries again. "Christmas spirit?"

I laugh. "Fine. You got yourself into this mess by doing a good deed, or trying to. So this is my good deed. One bonus event—and you're cashing it in on the Christmas tree lighting."

He sticks out his hand. "Deal."

"Deal," I say.

As we shake hands, the faint gingerbread scent of the soap my dad puts in the guest rooms wafts from his warm, calloused hands. Then I hear giggles and whispers on the other side of the kitchen door and drop his hand with a quickness. He cocks his head.

"My sisters are spying on us from the kitchen window."

He lifts his hand and waves. The laughter inside intensifies. I shake my head. We all used to peek through that window to watch each other say goodnight to our boyfriends on the porch. I guess *some* of us haven't matured.

I push open the door with a jangle of bells and lead him inside.

CHAPTER 12

THREE THINGS, THE SPEED ROUND

Jack

The kitchen's warm and bright. The tangy scent of freshly baked dough tickles my nose, and a pot of red sauce simmers on the stove. Soft holiday music plays but it's barely audible over the noise of the Jolly family's chatter. Noelle takes our coats, and Merry squeals and sweeps Holly into a big hug as Nick slaps my back in a hearty greeting.

Holly wriggles free from her youngest sister and pulls a slim, smiling woman toward me.

"Jack, this is my middle sister, Ivy. Ivy, meet Jack Bell, dastardly book donor."

Ivy ducks her head and laughs. "Hi, Jack. I'm the quiet Jolly. The *only* quiet Jolly. Consider yourself warned."

As if to prove her point, at this moment, Noelle says

something that causes Nick to roar with laughter and Merry to shriek. Holly shakes her head.

"Told ya. Do you guys want a drink before dinner?" Ivy asks, gesturing to the ice cube-filled glasses lined up on the island next to a pitcher of rose red liquid. "Noelle mixed up some Negronis."

I glance at Holly, planning to follow her cue. She grins. "Might as well celebrate closing our deal with a cocktail."

"Sounds good to me."

Nick pours the drinks and Ivy passes them around. Once everyone's holding a rocks glass garnished with an orange slice, Noelle suggests moving into the family room. I follow the family into a cozy room with overstuffed, comfortable-looking furniture arranged in a half-circle around a hearth. Logs crackle in the fireplace and fuzzy blankets are draped over the backs of chairs and arms of sofas. Wicker baskets full of books, puzzles, and games vie for space on the horizontal surfaces with fragrant candles and colorful nutcrackers. The room is decorated for Christmas, but it's homier and less grand than what I saw of the inn earlier. The word inviting springs to mind. I imagine the Jollys curled up here reading or playing board games as snow falls outside the mullioned windows.

Holly catches me looking around. "This is part of the family wing. No guests ever come back here. It's where we live. Or lived, I guess. Only Noelle and Dad live here year-round now."

I nod, but before I can respond, Nick raises his glass. "What should we drink to?"

"Holly and Jack have a deal to celebrate," Merry volunteers.

"A deal? You actually got Anderson to agree to a deal?" Noelle's agog.

Holly snorts. "As if. No, Jack and I reached a compromise with regard to all this Christmas crap." She waves her free hand around as if the crap in question is in the room.

"Holly Evelyn," her father scolds good-naturedly. "All this 'Christmas crap' is the lifeblood of our town."

She rolls her eyes, but Noelle butts in before she can get in her retort. "So what's the compromise?"

"Uncle Chris ordered that Jack can't attend any of the Christmas crap without me. And Jack and I agreed that we will go to a dozen holiday events of his choice over the course of the month."

"Uh-uh. Thirteen." I wink at Merry. "A baker's dozen—tonight's tree lighting plus twelve more."

Holly's family hoots. Well, Ivy titters. The rest of them hoot.

"Court-ordered Christmas cheer?" Nick jokes. "I'll drink to that."

"*Cin cin,*" Noelle says. A warm look passes between her and Nick at the Italian toast.

The Jollys and I clink glasses. I've always wondered what a normal family life would be like. Now, I'm getting a glimpse. Well, a glimpse of normal family life if the family lived in a holiday movie. But, it's close enough for me.

We make short work of the pitcher of Negronis and move into the dining room. The Jollys jabber and pass slices of pizza around the wide table family style. Someone opens a bottle of red wine. Holly disappears into the kitchen and returns with two liters of mineral water.

"Let's remember to alternate the booze with water, fam. We don't want a repeat of the tree lighting of 2021." She shoots a pointed look toward Merry, who dissolves into peals of laughter.

To my right, Ivy whispers, "Merry went a little hard at dinner that year. She regaled the crowd with a risqué rendition of 'Santa Baby' until we dragged her off the stage."

Holly leans over to confirm this tale. "True story. Poor Jamal was the tree-lighting Santa that year. I still don't think he's fully recovered."

Merry takes the glass of water her father hands her and sips it with dignity. "Haters gonna hate," she observes coolly.

The whole dinner is like this. The conversation and the wine flow easily. The sisters rib each other, Nick and Noelle interject with memories and funny stories, and every so often, someone lobs me a softball question about Florida or traveling.

When the pizzas have all been devoured, Holly announces, "We forgot to do three things."

Nick checks his watch. "We have time for a speed round. We need to gather the guests to walk over to the square."

Aware that I'm completely lost, Noelle catches my eye. "You'll figure it out, Jack. You can go last. Holly, you start."

"And … go." Nick presses a button on the side of his watch face that I assume sets a timer, then points at Holly. "One thing you're grateful for, one thing you regret, one thing you'll do to make tomorrow a better day."

Holly speaks in a rapid-fire cadence, "Noelle's Negronis, trusting Delphina to fill my coffee order, keep alternating water and wine."

Nick nods. "Merry, go."

"Jack convincing Holly to come to the tree lighting, missing my Pilates class with Griselda, make a double batch of gingerbread so I can get ahead of next week's orders."

"Noe, you're up."

Noelle ticks her statements off on her fingers, "The Bryants canceling so the guest house was free for Holly and Jack, running late after work because I didn't have time to stop by the post office and mail out the holiday cards like I said I would, spend some time coming up with a fresh spin on this year's Bookmas event. Your turn, Nick."

"Merry teaching me how to finally twirl pizza dough like a pro, ignoring Noelle's advice to wear gloves when I carried in the firewood and having to pick a hundred splinters out of my hands, train Josh Morgenthal as a backup Santa so he can visit the Stillwater animal rescue for pictures with adoptable pets. Ivy?"

Ivy's mouth curves into a grin and she catches Noelle's eye. "Grabbing that stack of cards from the reception desk and popping them in the mail during my morning walk, eating nothing but marshmallow brownies and chocolate peppermints for lunch, help mend costumes and repair the sets for the Nutcracker ballet."

Noelle mouths 'thank you' to Ivy while Nick gestures toward me.

I clear my throat. "Weird as it sounds, I'm glad I stopped in this town, I regret not driving a harder bargain with Holly on the holiday events, and I plan to steer clear of little free libraries." I finish just as Nick's watch begins beeping.

We push back our chairs and clear the table. The family moves in choreographed unison, and I try to stay out of their way. Within minutes, the dishes are rinsed and arranged in the dishwasher, the table is wiped down and the chairs pushed in, and the kitchen is spotless. We put on our coats and follow Nick and Noelle through the hallway to the reception lobby, where guests are gathering in clusters.

"Does your family do that every night—the three things?" I ask Holly as we lag behind the group.

"Yep. Well, not the speed round. We usually all do the thing we're thankful for in detail and ask questions of each other, then repeat the process for the other two. It's a leisurely discussion. But, yes, we did it every night with our mom and dad growing up. And now Dad and Noelle do it, and we join in when we're together as a family." She pulls a pair of gloves from her coat pockets and wriggles her hands into them. "Why?"

I shrug. "It's nice. That's all."

"Does your family have any traditions like that?"

"Not really. When my dad took off, my mom had a four-year-old and a three-year-old to take care of with no family nearby to help her. She worked. A lot. For years, she worked a nine-to-five, picked me and my older brother up at the afterschool program, fed us, bathed us, helped us with our homework, and put us to bed. Then she had a side hustle from home that she worked on late into the night. Lots of times, we'd come downstairs in the morning and she'd be sound asleep at the kitchen table with her head resting on her arms."

She's quiet for a moment. "I'm sorry. That sounds hard—for all of you."

I shrug again. "I'm making it sound grimmer than it was. We didn't have a lot of extra money or time. But she loved us as hard as she could, read to us every night, came up with free, fun things we could do on the weekends. She always had our backs. She was our biggest cheerleader. I have a lot of good memories from those times." I laugh bitterly. "When we were teens, our financial situation improved—a lot. Her side hustle took off, I mean, really took off. For the first time, she had—we had—breathing room." I fall silent for a moment, my stomach twisting and sour, before I say, "But then she met Roger."

I know she's about to ask me about Roger, and the last thing I want to do is talk about my prick of a stepfather. Luckily, a slow, lazy snowflake picks that moment to land on her cheek. She squeaks in surprise, and I brush it off with two fingers.

"It's *snowing!*" she calls to the others, clapping her gloved hands together like a little girl. Then she turns back to me, her eyes shining. "Looks like you're going to have your second white Christmas ever."

I can't help smiling at the flush of excitement on her face as flakes continue to fall, dusting our hair and collars. "Looks like."

"I love it when it snows during the tree lighting," she breathes as she grabs my hand in hers and pulls me along to catch up with her family and their guests.

CHAPTER 13

LIGHTS, AMBER ALE, ILL-ADVISED ACTION

Holly

For all my grumbling about the tree lighting, it's probably my favorite Mistletoe Mountain holiday tradition. Or at least it was until two years ago, when Anderson dropped to one knee in front of the entire town and asked me to marry him. I'll admit, I was over the moon to marry him, but I would have preferred a more private proposal—especially coming just a year after Merry's "Santa Baby" performance.

But Anderson loves the spotlight, and getting engaged in front of the town's spectacular tree was a surefire way to garner attention. It helped that he tipped off the local newspaper and an engagement and wedding photographer from Virginia who managed to get a shot of our magical moment placed in a glossy magazine read by all his mom's friends at the Loudon Horse and Country Club. (Did I fantasize about sending *The Elegant Horsewoman* a blind item about their favorite native son's adulterous ways? Yes. But Ivy stopped me before I could do it.)

In contrast to the hot glare of hundreds of pairs of eyes on me, last year's tree lighting is nothing more than a vague, slightly fuzzy, sepia-toned image in my mind. It was the first Christmas after my mom died, before Noelle rescued my dad—and us—from our miasma of grief (although she'd argue he did the rescuing). Anderson was by my side, I know that much. But beyond that? I assume the tree was lit, songs were sung, and cheer filled the air.

I'm jostled out of my admittedly morose memories by an excited tug on my sleeve. "You came!"

I turn to see Delphina, who's lost the elf hat but still sports the ornament earrings. They bounce off her shoulders as she pulls me into a tight hug and squeezes me.

"I came," I admit, hugging her back.

Her eyes widen as her gaze lands on Jack. "And you brought … a date?"

"Jack is a client," I quickly correct her. "It's a long story."

One of her impeccably threaded eyebrows quirks. "Sure." Then she reaches behind her and drags a large, muscular guy forward. "This is my date, Titus. Titus, this is my bestie, Holly. And her *client*, Jack."

Titus drapes one arm over her shoulder. "Charmed."

Noelle leans in to peer at him. "I know you. You're the bartender from Dancing Ladies."

Titus grins. "Guilty as charged."

"Dancing Ladies?" Jack asks.

"Strip bar," Ivy explains.

"It's a gentlemen's club with exotic dancers," Dad corrects her. Ever since he joined the town's motorcycle club, his views have really evolved.

"I need a drink," Ivy whispers.

"Amen to that. Delph, tell me you brought your flask?" I flash her a hopeful smile.

"Sorry, sister. I came straight from the coffee shop."

I shoot Merry a look, but she shakes her head. "After the lecture I got about pacing myself and water? Are you for real right now?"

"Ah, the 'Santa Baby' debacle of '21," Delphina says fondly. "Good times."

"Don't worry," Titus tells me, leaning forward conspiratorially. "Frosty Brewery is sponsoring a beer garden after the lighting—big heated tent, the whole works."

I wrinkle my nose. "Mmm, I don't like beer."

My best friend and sisters exchange a *look*. Not just a look, a *look*. It's laden with subtext and unspoken agreement.

"What?" I demand.

Ivy's eyes slide to the ground. Merry examines her nails.

Delphina sighs. "Really, you two? You're going to throw me under the sleigh?"

Noelle clears her throat and places a hand on Delph's

arm. "I'll field this." She fixes me with her emerald green eyes.

When she speaks, her voice is soft and her tone is kind. But her words cut me to the quick. "Holly, honey, you actually *do* like beer. Or you did. But you spent so long being told what you did and did not like that I—we—think you may have lost sight of your own preferences."

My cheeks heat and my pulse races as I realize she's right. I look up at the cold sky and let the snow hit my face, hoping it will fend off the hot tears pricking behind my eyes. Anderson is the one who doesn't like beer. Correction, he likes beer just fine. He didn't like it for me. He didn't want his future wife to be seen guzzling from a bottle. Even drinking an overpriced IPA from a glass was unseemly. It would make me look unsophisticated.

Why in the name of all that is hoppy and delicious had I listened to him? The answer comes immediately: because I'd rather accede to his dumb, but ultimately, unimportant request than admit that I was wrong about him, wrong about us. The problem with that plan was the unimportant requests piled up, I never asserted myself because I wanted to keep the peace, and he still cheated on me in a public display that left no doubt how very wrong I'd been.

I fill my lungs with cold, crisp air and breathe out slowly. When I've successfully reigned in my emotions, I turn back to Titus. "A beer garden, huh? So long as they're serving their amber ale count me in."

My sisters and Delphina whoop and squeal loudly

enough to draw attention. I feel the eyes on my back and turn to see Anderson and Tabitha talking to a wildly gesticulating Vicky Swanson. I shoot them a wide smile. Anderson and Mrs. Swanson give me twin frowns but Tabitha returns my smile with a tiny one of her own. I look away quickly. She was my boss, but I also considered her a mentor and, stupidly, a friend. She was clearly not that.

"Hope you like beer," I whisper to Jack.

"I'm easy," he whispers back. "My motto is roll with it. So sure, the beer garden sounds like fun."

Roll with it. Who *is* this man, and more importantly, what's *that* like?

Before I can inquire more about Jack's life philosophy, Dawn Min, our town manager, takes the stage in front of a towering white pine. She waves to the crowd and flips on the microphone.

"Welcome everyone, to the annual Christmas tree lighting! How about this snow?" She grins, and people start clapping and hooting. "We couldn't have asked for a better night to kick off Merriment Month in Mistletoe Mountain! We'll get to it, but first I have a few quick announcements." She checks her notes. "First, let's hear it for Pete Swanson, who went out to White Pines Tree Farm to bring back the fabulous tree we're about to light."

"Thanks, Pete!" A shout goes up from somewhere in the crowd.

Mr. Swanson, wearing a plaid hat with ear flaps, raises one hand in acknowledgement. He's standing with Clem

Stillwater and some other friends rather than his wife and the DA and her boy toy (as Delph likes to call Anderson). I have to wonder if Pete agrees with Vicky's latest crusade.

"New this year, we have a beer garden courtesy of the Frosty Brewery. It's located beside the chapel, in the lot in front of Marley Jacobs' law offices. In addition to Frosty's full lineup of beers, they'll be serving handcrafted root beer for the little ones. Speaking of Attorney Jacobs, she's sponsoring Sober Sleigh rides home for anyone who's not walking. And finally, our sincere thanks to the merchants and business owners who make up our chamber of commerce for funding this display and so many of our other events. Now, without further ado, let's get this party started!"

She signals the Mapleville Merrymakers, and the band strikes up a steel-drum version of "Rocking Around the Christmas Tree." Then her adorable, precocious daughter Sunny hits the oversized switch, and the majestic tree lights up in a burst of color to enormous applause. A moment later, the intricately decorated street lamps that line the square turn on and white lights outline leaping reindeer along all four streets. Santa's gazebo is next. The lighted snowflakes hanging from the roof twinkle on, all while the band plays, the crowd sways, and the snow softly falls. Beside me, Jack sighs a mixture of contentment and amazement, and I smile to myself. Despite my reluctance, I'm so grateful to be here, in this place, at this moment.

The crowd breaks up and people start drifting off in pairs and groups. Griselda comes over to Dad and Noelle.

"Some of us are going to the North Pole Social Club," she tells them. "Care to join?"

"You're not going to the beer garden?" Merry asks.

Griselda waves a hand. "Speaking only for myself, I'm too old to trade comfort for free beer. I'd rather pay for my drinks and have them indoors."

Noelle giggles. "Sign me up."

Dad gives us a playful finger wag. "Have fun at the beer garden—but not too much fun. Remember, we're going to get our tree tomorrow afternoon when Noelle's done at the library. So I need everyone to be fully functioning."

"Have fun," I call as Dad, Noelle, and Griselda melt into the crowd streaming away from the square and walk toward High Street. I catch myself flicking my gaze over to Anderson and Tabitha. Presumably they'll also trade comfort for free booze, and I won't have to worry about running into them in the beer garden. At least I hope so, because this is the first time I've been in a social situation with the two of them since I stumbled on their adult version of Five Minutes in the Closet.

Jack asks Titus a question about his tattoo, and Delphina uses the opportunity to pull me aside, looping her elbow through mine.

"He's your client?"

"Yes."

"And Anderson is on the other side of the case?"

"Also, yes. By the way, he wants to be called Anders."

She snorts. "Yeah, good luck with that."

And this is one of the million reasons why I love Delph.

"So how long have you been dating Titus?"

"We're not dating. He's my date."

"What's the difference?"

She sighs. "I know it's been a while, but you go *on dates* with someone to decide whether you want *to date* them in a more long-term fashion."

"Got it. Is this your first date?"

"I know him from Dancing Ladies and we've been talking for a while. But it's been more of a business mentorship because he's interested in opening his own small business. So yes, this is our first date-date."

"What kind of business does he want to open?" I'm thinking maybe a record shop or a piercing studio. Possibly a tattoo parlor.

"A cat cafe."

"A *cat* cafe?"

"Yeah, he plans to partner with the animal rescue to sponsor adoptable cats. And since he's going to specialize in tea service, it won't cut into my business."

"Or, hear me out, he could serve *actual* coffee, which would also not compete with the Snowflake Cafe."

In response, she pinches my arm playfully. "I'll ignore that since I'm so happy to see you out and about."

"You can thank Jack and Judge MacIntosh for that."

"Come again?"

"Jack was charged with unlawful trespass for putting some books in Mrs. Swanson's Little Free Library. Tabitha must have been out of the office when the police picked him up—she usually goes shopping with her sisters on Black Friday. The best I can figure is she left Anderson in charge, and he decided to bring criminal charges."

She stops walking and yanks me backward. "You're kidding."

"I wish."

"Anyway, Anderson requested no bail, and rather than let Jack sit in county lockup until after the holidays, Judge McIntosh remanded him into my custody."

"Your place is miniscule. What are you going to do with him? Make a bed on your kitchen counter?"

I laugh. "It's not *that* small, but we're staying at the guest house at the inn."

Her eyes widen. "How?"

"The Bryants canceled at the last minute so Dad said we could have it. There's only one bed, but we'll work it out."

"What you should work out is having a fling with a hot out-of-towner."

I'm shaking my head before she finishes the sentence. "No way. That would be messy for a lot of reasons."

"Name one."

"He's my client."

"Okay, name another one."

"I'm not ready."

"You don't need to be ready to have a fling."

Luckily, we reach the entrance to the beer garden and she drops the topic.

❄

hree Christmas ales later, I'm reminded that I really do like beer. I'm also slightly past tipsy. Merry slides a glass of water in front of me, and I give her a woozy smile. "Thanks."

"Don't mention it," she says before returning to her good-natured argument with one of the Marino brothers about active yeast versus sourdough starter.

Ivy got swept away by a group of her friends as soon as we walked in the doors. Last time I saw her, she was dancing. And now Delphina and Titus have joined the dancers, which leaves just me and Jack at the table we snagged right under a heater.

I turn to him. "So, what do you think?"

His eyes crinkle. "About?"

I wave a hand. "All of it. The beer garden, the lighting, the town, the people."

He takes his time responding, sipping his lager. "I think," he says, then his eyes flick over my shoulder and whatever he was about to say dies in his throat. He looks down into his glass and says, "That ADA just walked in."

My chest tightens and I steel myself before I turn around to see Tabitha, impossible to miss in her long scarlet coat, with Anderson standing stiffly beside her, looking like he wishes he was anywhere but here. His obvious discomfort sparks a tiny bit of joy in me.

"Let's dance," I say brightly.

Surprise flashes in Jack's eyes, then he shrugs. I'm guessing his internal monologue is *roll with it*, because he drains his beer and says, "Sure."

He takes my outstretched hand and I lead him to the temporary parquet dance floor that's been put down in one corner of the tent.

Delphina gives me a surprised look of approval as we join the dancers, and Ivy flashes me a completely cheesy and not at all discreet thumbs up. I start moving to the beat and I swear I can feel Anderson's eyes boring into my back. I ignore the feeling of being watched and focus on the music. I love to dance, but much like beer, my ex-fiancé found it unseemly. I raise my arms over my head and shake it off. Jack moves his hips with mesmerizing grace, smiling the whole time.

The song ends and the DJ puts on a slow dance. Ivy and her friends filter over to the table. Delphina wraps her arms around Titus's neck and they start swaying back and forth.

I give Jack an uncertain look and he holds out his hand. I hesitate, but only for a nanosecond, before I take it. He pulls me close and presses our clasped hands to his chest.

He's tall enough that even in my heeled boots, I can rest my head on his shoulder. We turn and my hip brushes against his. Heat crackles through me.

In my peripheral vision, I see Anderson leading Tabitha to the floor. I turn away, looking up at Jack. His bright blue eyes darken as he looks down at me, and my breath hitches.

He cups the side of my head then runs his big hand over my hair to my cheek and then down to my collarbone, and I take a deep, shaky breath. We're barely moving now.

He lowers his cheek to mine, and the scratch of his beard rubs against my skin.

"Holly," his voice is a rasp. "I'm going to kiss you now, unless you say not to."

I swallow hard, my heart a trapped bird in my chest. "Kiss me," I say.

He dips his head to drop a series of soft, fluttering kisses along my clavicle before tilting my chin up with two fingers and covering my mouth with his. My lips part, yielding to the firm pressure as he kisses me hard. I press against him, desperate to get closer.

I don't realize that we've stopped moving until someone jostles us from the side. It breaks whatever spell we've fallen under, and he removes his mouth from mine. I feel the absence acutely.

"Sorry," he says to the dancers who've collided with us.

Then he turns to me. "Why don't we sit?" he rumbles deep in his throat.

He leads me off the floor, back to our table where we sit, side by side, our fingers still entwined. He rubs the underside of my wrist with his thumb, and I shiver with need and desire.

Then as suddenly as I lost myself in his kiss, my head

clears. A wave of horror washes over me. I'm flooded with shame. I ease my hand out from his and grab my water glass.

I drain it in one swallow before I say, "I'm so sorry."

"For what?"

"For *that*." I gesture toward the dance floor. "It was completely inappropriate. I'm your lawyer."

"We're both adults, Holly."

"It's unethical, Jack."

He shakes his head. "I don't understand."

"I don't know what came over me." This is a lie—I do know what came over me. I'm wildly attracted to this man.

"Holly—" he begins.

I cut him off. "Hold that thought. I need to use the bathroom."

He frowns skeptically, but it happens to be true. I suddenly desperately need to pee. Eight hundred glasses of water will do that to a girl.

As I weave my way through the crowd, I run into Merry and Ivy.

"We were looking for you. A bunch of us are going to Rudy's for late-night cheese fries and greasy burgers. Do you and Jack wanna join?" Ivy asked.

"Oh, no, but thanks."

"Are you sure? We've already called the Sober Sleigh. Delphina and Titus are coming."

"I think we're done for the night."

My sisters exchange a knowing look.

"Got it," Merry smirks.

"It's not like that."

"You sure about that? You guys looked pretty cozy on the dance floor." Ivy raises an eyebrow.

"He's my client. There are rules of conduct."

Merry scoffs. "Live a little. You don't have to follow *every* rule."

I gape at my youngest sister as if she's speaking a foreign language. "I really do." Before she can argue I say, "Listen, have fun at Rudy's. I'll see you tomorrow when we go get the tree."

We share a quick hug and I wend my way to the corridor where the line for the ladies room starts. The line inches forward, and right as I reach the front, the door swings open and Delphina walks out.

"Saw you kissing," she says without preamble.

"Bladder's gonna burst," I respond.

She sighs. "Fine. We can debrief at Rudy's."

I shake my head. "Jack and I are done for the night. Talk tomorrow?"

"Talk tomorrow."

She gives me a quick peck on the cheek and I rush into the bathroom.

After I use the facilities, I take my time washing and drying my hands. Then I touch up my lipstick, which has been kissed off. My lips are tender, almost raw and I picture Jack's demanding mouth.

On my way back to the table, someone grabs my elbow.

I wheel around to see Anderson.

"Let go of me."

"I saw you, Holly. You're completely out of line."

He's right, I know he's right. But instead of admitting as much, I stiffen my spine. Who is he to tell me what I can and cannot do? My temper rises. "It's none of your business, Anderson."

"Oh, that's where you're wrong. As your opposing counsel, I'm not going to have this case thrown out because you've violated your ethical obligations to your client."

I laugh. "You want to file a bar complaint, Anderson? Go right ahead. I'll counter it with one of my own."

"My ethics are above reproach," he scoffs.

"You think so? I wonder how the taxpayers would feel knowing the district attorney's office is a hotbed of sex."

His nostrils flare and his face reddens. "You wouldn't." His voice is loud, almost, but not quite, a shout.

"Try me," I say evenly.

Tabitha races over and places a hand on Anderson's arm. "Anders, it's time to go."

"You heard the boss. Bye-bye."

He holds my gaze for a moment longer before turning away.

Tabitha gives me an apologetic smile as she leads him away.

I wait until they're halfway across the tent before I walk over to Jack, my legs shaking from the confrontation. My mouth is dry and my heart is racing. Of all people, it had to be Anderson who voiced the professional concerns already gnawing at my conscience. Even worse, he's right, though I'd rather eat fruitcake than admit it to him.

"Are you okay?" Jack asks, rising halfway from his chair when he sees my face. "What was that all about?"

I drop into my seat, the pleasant buzz from the Christmas ales completely gone now, replaced by a knot in my stomach. The warmth of his kiss lingers on my lips, which feels like an indictment. "Nothing," I say, then I stop myself. "No, not nothing. Anderson threatened to report me to the bar."

The muscle in Jack's jaw tightens. "Over a consensual kiss?"

His indignation would be sweet if it weren't so misplaced. I've worked so hard to build my professional reputation. A moment of weakness—delicious as it was—isn't worth risking my career.

"There are rules, Jack."

"Well, they're crap."

I sigh. I don't really want to sit here and explain the rules of professional conduct in the middle of a raging party. "Let's just—can we go back to the cottage?"

For a moment, I think he's going to object, but he doesn't. "Yeah, sure. I'll get our coats."

We walk back in silence under the twinkling lights. The only sound is the faint music from the tent and the crunch of the snow under our feet. My mind whirrs as I try to figure out what to say, how to make this not awkward.

On the porch, before I tap in the code to unlock the door, I turn to him. "I want you to know it's not that I didn't like kissing you."

He parses the double negative, and his mouth quirks up. "Oh, I could tell you liked it."

My pulse races and I look away from his mouth. "But it's complicated."

I unlock the door and push it open. He follows me inside and we stomp the snow off our shoes on the mat in the entryway.

"It's only complicated if you make it complicated," he tells me.

I am suddenly bone-tired and weary. I slip out of my boots and walk into the kitchen to pour us each a large glass of water. I hand him one. "We'll have to agree to disagree, at least for now. I'm exhausted."

He leans against the island and holds my gaze for a beat. Then he tips the water glass toward me. "Cheers."

My fingers itch to rake through his thick hair and tug him toward me so I can cover his mouth with my bruised and swollen lips. Instead, I take a long drink.

He drains his glass, places it in the sink, and brushes past me, heading toward the sofa.

"No, take the bedroom. I told you, you're a guest."

He turns and shoots me a look. "And I'm not letting you sleep on this couch."

I throw up my hands. "How about this? We'll alternate. You take the bed tonight. I'll sleep there tomorrow. I don't want to stay up and argue about this. I really want to get some sleep. Please."

"Have it your way," he says with a shrug before heading toward the bedroom. He pauses at the threshold and gives me a long, searing look. "Sweet dreams, Holly."

"Good night, Jack."

CHAPTER 14

THE NICKNAME IT DESERVES

Jack

Sunlight stabs through the gap in the blackout blinds that cover the wide windows. I raised them last night to admire the moon shining on the snow and, like a moron, didn't pull them all the way back down. So now, my mild hangover is exacerbated by the bright morning light. I groan and fling an arm over my eyes then listen hard to determine if Holly is up and moving around in the living room. There are no sounds to suggest she's up and about. There are also no sounds to suggest she's still asleep on the couch. If anything, the cottage feels empty.

I sit up with another groan, swing my legs around, and miss the throw rug by the side of the bed, planting my bare feet on the chilly wood floor. The sensation jolts me wide awake, and in the cold, hard, headache-inducing light of day, the memory of kissing Holly rushes back.

I have no regrets. Not a single one. The corollary to *roll with it* is *shoot your shot,* and I'm willing to take a chance when I feel a connection with someone. Sometimes it works, sometimes it doesn't. But this, this feels different.

Yes, I'd just met her. But the way our bodies fit together dancing, like two interlocking puzzle pieces, the weight of her head nestled on my shoulder, the heat of her breath on my neck made it feel right. No, it made it feel inevitable. And the feel of her mouth under mine, her hips pressing into me did nothing to refute that feeling. We have a connection and whether it scares her or she really is hampered by some rule, Holly felt it too. I know she did. The question is, what am I going to do about it?

I run my fingers through my hair and scrub a hand over my beard. I should've insisted that she take the bed last night. But, while she was too tired to continue the conversation, I was too turned-on. Even after she pulled away, even after the bracing walk home through the snow. I was ready to take her to bed, not just give her the bed. So I mustered all my self-control and walked through the bedroom door, alone. I'm not sure I can do it thirty-four more times, though.

I shove the thought of Holly to the far recesses of my brain, pull on a t-shirt, and pad into the bathroom to splash some water on my face, and brush my teeth. I squint at my reflection in the mirror. I look better than I feel. Or, at least, not worse.

On my way back through the bedroom, I catch the unmistakable scent of coffee and smile to myself—Holly's up after all. I dig a pair of sweatpants out of my backpack and pull them over my boxers, run my hands through my hair, and open the bedroom door prepared to greet her.

The cottage is empty, but I hadn't imagined the scent of coffee. There's a silver carafe on the island holding down a note scribbled on a notepad with a poinsettia border.

> Jack,
> I went for a run. Coffee's hot. Enjoy your day. We leave for the tree farm at 2. - Holly
> P.S. Tree farm is not an official holiday activity on the calendar, but you're welcome to join us if you like.

I reread the note as I pour myself a mug of coffee from the carafe and dig into Merry's treats for my breakfast. This note gives mixed messages. One, she's gone already, which is either evidence that she's an early morning runner or that she's avoiding me. I don't know her well enough to know, but being an early morning runner, even the day after a night out, fits her personality, so I put that piece of evidence aside as inconclusive.

Two, she clearly told me I'm on my own for the day. Could be looking to put some distance between us. Could just be busy. Inconclusive. But, three, she *did* invite me to join her family to cut down their tree. That seems very much like a personal overture, but she could just be being polite—as she reminded me yesterday, she is the daughter of an innkeeper. Again, inconclusive. I toss the note back on the counter, pour myself another mug of coffee, and eat two cinnamon stars and an anise-flavored pizzelle.

Ten minutes later, I've changed into jeans and am striding down High Street. I'm pretty sure I'm headed in the direction of the library. If not, I'm sure I'll find something else to pass the time, so long as I stay away from the official activities so I don't run afoul of the judge's order. Once I pass the jewelry store and the social club, I know I'm going the right way and quicken my pace.

I stop in front of the library. From the front, it looks like a whimsical gingerbread house, tall and thin. But once inside, the space opens with loads of glass, soaring ceilings and gleaming white walls. I only saw it from the back yesterday when we dropped off the books, but the instant I walk through the doors I know this place is the heart of the community.

My initial impression is confirmed. There's a tool-lending library, a seed library, and a display about tapping sugar maples. There are board games and toys to borrow, a room with video game systems, and a teen lounge with bean bags. There's a sign for a children's wing to the left and for a makerspace upstairs, but, above all, there are books. Towering floor-to-ceiling shelves of books. I rest my hand on one and realize the glass block bookshelves function as support beams for the building. This library is literally built on books. I catch myself grinning.

"Hey, Jack!"

I turn around at my name to see Noelle waving to me from behind a book cart.

"Morning," I say.

"Is it?" she asks. "I got a text from Merry at three-thirty this morning. Sounded like the party went late."

My grin falters. "Holly and I didn't go out after the beer garden. We headed back to the cottage."

"Did you enjoy your first night of Mistletoe Mountain social life?"

Unbidden, the image of Holly's eyes shining up at me, her lips parted, fills my mind.

"I did," I choke out.

"So, can I help you find something in particular?"

"No, I'm just killing time. Holly's out for a run and I'm on my own until you all head to the Christmas tree farm. She invited me to tag along. I hope that's okay."

"Of course! You're gonna love it." She pauses. "Did your family decorate a Christmas tree back in Florida?"

I laugh. "Fake trees all the way."

"Oh, well then you're *really* gonna love the Christmas tree farm." Noelle laughs with delight. "In the meantime, I can show you around the library or press a volunteer into service, if you like. It's really something."

"I can see that," I tell her. "I've been to a lot of libraries. I can already tell yours is a standout. But, I'm good to just wander on my own."

Her cheeks flush with pride. "Thanks. Well, make sure you pop into our children's wing. It's one of a kind."

"I will," I promise.

She's about to walk away when a thought occurs to me. "Do you have any law books?"

She wrinkles her forehead. "Are you researching your case? Really, Holly's an excellent attorney. You don't need to do that."

"No, I just have a very specific question about the rules of professional conduct."

Noelle blinks, and I can see her curiosity warring with professionalism. The librarian wins out, and she doesn't ask for any details. Instead, she says, "There's an alcove on the second floor in the back right corner that functions as the county law library. Once most people moved to online research, the bar association didn't want to maintain a physical library anymore, so we adopted it for them. The case reporters may not all be up to date, but I know the rule books are. I can show you where it is."

"I'll find it," I assure her.

And I do. I follow her directions to a quiet corner on the second floor where two built-in bookcases flank a tall window with comfortable reading chairs positioned to capture the natural light. I run my finger along the book spines until I reach a volume titled *Vermont Rules of Court*. I grab the book off the shelf, flip through it until I find the section labeled "Rules of Professional Conduct," and sink into a chair to scan the mind-numbing legal verbiage. Rule 1.8 must be the one Holly's hung up on. I read the section, then read it again more slowly.

I stand and return the book to its shelf, frowning in thought. Holly wasn't exaggerating; starting a "sexual relationship" with a current client is explicitly forbidden. But the rule says nothing about what's allowed after the representation ends. I file these details away and stretch, ready to explore the rest of the charming library.

I wander around for a while then make my way toward the reception desk. I'd spotted the director's office behind it earlier and figure I can find Noelle in there. Instead, she's sitting behind the desk with a box full of books spread out on the table. I recognize the titles instantly. She looks up as I approach, puts aside the copy of *Fahrenheit 451*, and smiles expectantly.

"Well, what'd you think? Find everything you were looking for?"

"I did, and then I spent some time checking out the library. I wish there'd been a library like this when I was growing up. The makerspace is extremely cool. But that children's wing is something else. There's an impromptu puppet show going on, and some little guy is hustling people at the chessboard."

She roars with laughter. "Brent Stillwater, the town chess prodigy," she tells me. "They must be tourists because everybody around here knows better than to get into a game with Brent. He's not playing for money again, is he?"

"Looked like candy canes."

"Hmm, that's marginally better, I guess."

I point my chin at the books on the table. "How can people think reading is so dangerous?"

Her voice grows serious, "People fear ideas. They're afraid of their children being exposed to different perspectives and questioning what they've been taught. It's so sad."

She picks up a book and brandishes it at me. "I mean, look at this. Have you read *The Sign of the Olive and the Dove?* It's the first book in Jackie Samuel's YA resistance dystopian series. She's brilliant. *It's* brilliant. But it's been banned all over the place because it teaches kids to defy authority." She shakes her head and sighs. "They plot to overthrow the government."

This conversation hits a little too close for comfort, so I change the subject. "Last night, you said that you have a Bookmas event to run. What are you planning?"

"I wish I knew," she says absently, still tapping the book cover. "Every year we do something literature-related to tie into the festivities. We've done Christmas classics, a book and a movie, a few different 'twelve days of' themes, but this year we only have one day on the calendar, so I need to make it count."

I pull the calendar in question from my pocket and smooth it over the table. I point to a date two weeks in the future labeled "To Be Determined Book Event at the Library." "This one?"

"That's it," she confirms.

Her eyes flick back to the books on the table. "I wonder," she rubs her chin, "if there's something we could do with these books to tie in to the importance of standing up to book bans."

I snap my fingers. "Banned book bingo."

A smile crosses her face. "Banned book bingo—I love it!"

"I can't claim credit. A few different advocacy groups have done some version of it. But maybe there's a way to make it holiday themed."

She waves a hand. "Believe me, you can turn anything into a holiday theme in Mistletoe Mountain—the prizes, decorations, music will all carry the theme. Banned book bingo it is!"

"I'd be happy to help you with it," I say. "Obviously, this is an issue I care about, and I have nothing but time. Plus you can give some of my books as prizes, too."

"Oh, Jack, I welcome your help, for sure. But, you don't need to donate books. I have a budget for this."

"Please. I'm probably going to be gun-shy about sticking them in people's libraries once I get my criminal matter cleared up."

We're chuckling at the absurdity of my criminal matter, when a teenager runs straight toward us, her headscarf streaming behind her.

"Noelle!" she pants, screeching to a halt in front of the reception desk.

Noelle's eyebrows furrow. "Farah? What's wrong?"

The girl takes a breath. "I was leading the preteen art project when Mrs. Swanson came stomping in and thrust these at me. She told me I *have* to hang them up."

She passes a pile of flyers to Noelle. I lean over her shoulder, and we read them together. In neat letters, someone has written with a thick marker, "Citizens Upholding Normal Traditions!" with a hand-drawn pile of books with an X over them. Under the drawing, there's a line listing the date, time, and place of the first meeting of "concerned citizens against inappropriate books."

Noelle begins to giggle.

I shoot her a look. "What's so funny?"

The giggle turns into full-blown laughter as she points to the flyer. "**C**itizens **U**pholding **N**ormal **T**raditions!"

"Right, so?" Farah gives her a worried look.

"The first letter of each word is bold. Once you see it, you won't be able to unsee it."

"Oh! Oh, no!" Farah's eyes go wide, and her hand flies up to cover her mouth.

"Oh, yes!" Noelle manages between cackles.

"I can't put these up," Farah says.

"Oh, we're putting them up. Vicky's right. The bulletin boards are designated for publicizing community events. As long as the event in question doesn't violate our anti-harassment policy, we're obligated to post the announcement." She wipes a tear from her eye. "Do me a favor, though. Make sure you post these prominently around the tween and teen rooms."

"Why?" Farah asks.

Noelle cuts me a sly look. "I want to make sure Vicky's group gets the nickname it deserves. And I know I can count on the young people to do that."

A reluctant giggle escapes from Farah's mouth, and she clutches the stack of papers to her chest. "Okay, Noelle."

We watch her leave, and then Noelle collapses into a fresh round of laughter. I smile, too, but I have an ominous feeling about this concerned citizen group, despite its oddly appropriate and hilarious name.

CHAPTER 15

FINDING WABI-SABI

Holly

My five-mile run stretches into a ten-miler as my thoughts churn. The cold air settles my sour stomach and my muscles warm up quickly, as I follow the road out of town and swing left on Lake Road. At the bend, I pause in front of the pair of stone lions. They guard the gate at the Swansons' place. I can see Vicky's little free library, clearly visible from the road. Painted the same buttery shade of yellow as the shingles and shutters on the Swansons' rancher, the box is on a post set in the middle of her garden, abloom with brilliant winterberry holly bushes.

As Jack noted, there isn't a no trespassing sign. Or a locked gate. Nothing at all visible from the road to suggest the Swansons don't want anyone to access the little free library in the garden. If I squint, I can just make out the little plaque on the library that I assume instructs visitors to ring the bell to unlock the library. But the box *wasn't* locked, so what's the legal basis for charging Jack?

I know even as I ask myself the question that there is none. Anderson saw an opportunity to get some press and make a name for himself, so he did. Criminal cases are far and few between around here, and he wasn't about to let the facts stand in the way of this one. It's as simple and cynical as that. The worst part is, I get it. I don't condone it, but I do understand his thinking.

I huff out a breath that hangs in the cold air, readjust my fleece headband, and start running again, working out the first stage of Jack's defense as my long legs churn over the pavement. I reach Snow Lake and do the circle around the outside, watching the lamentation of swans glide gracefully across the water. It turns out Snow Lake, despite its name, doesn't freeze in the winter because there's a natural hot spring underneath it. So the swans enjoy year-round swimming.

The weak winter sun glints off their downy white feathers as they skate over the water. Steam rises in dancing ribbons as the cold air meets the surface of the spring-fed lake. The snow piled high around the lake glitters like diamonds. I breathe, taking it in all. And then I return to my ruminating.

The sad truth is that all my legal strategizing, all the miles I've run, and all the natural beauty and wildlife I've admired can only distract me for so long. Eventually my mind returns to Jack. Jack, and our kiss. I fell asleep thinking about the kiss, and I woke up this morning thinking about it. I can't believe I did it. To say it's out of character for me to make out with a near-stranger in public is an understatement on par with saying kids are mildly interested in talking to the big guy in the red suit.

Did I do it to make Anderson jealous? I consider this possibility seriously, without judging myself, and decide that wasn't my motivation. I'd be lying if I said I didn't hope Anderson regretted throwing away a five-year relationship for some action in a closet. But Anderson Wilson Carson most definitely was *not* on my mind when Jack told me he was going to kiss me. What was on my mind was the pressure of Jack's broad, warm hands on my back, the way his eyes darkened with desire, the fit of my body against his, and the clean, grassy smell of his skin under the gingerbread-scented soap. I wanted to feel the press of his lips against mine. It was a moment of pure, raw want. And the heat that flares in my belly just thinking about it makes it clear that want hasn't gone away.

And if it weren't for professional rules of conduct, I'd want more. But there's no point in going down this path because the rules do exist. And while I hate to give credence to anything that comes out of Anderson's mouth, he's right: not only is it inappropriate to pursue anything with Jack, it's a poor legal strategy.

I speed up as I cross the hill and loop back around

toward town, pushing myself harder as if I'll be able to outrun my thoughts, outrun this desire, if I only move fast enough.

By the time I reach the cottage, my legs are limp noodles, my hair is sweaty under the headband, and my face is windburned. But the thought of kissing Jack is still lodged in my brain. So much for *that* plan. I did get a decent workout out of it, though.

I punch in the door code, let myself in, and find a note from Jack scribbled on the back of the one I left for him:

Went to the library. Back in time for the tree farm.

I do a quick cool-down stretch, guzzle some water, then eat a bowl of yogurt and granola while standing over the sink. If I were in my loft, I'd strip my stinky running tights and base layer off right here in the kitchen, but Jack could come home at any moment. So I push open the bedroom door to head into the attached bathroom.

I pause just inside the bedroom door. I feel like I'm trespassing, which is silly, I know. But it feels like a violation of Jack's privacy. I resolve to walk through the room as quickly as I can without snooping but can't help but notice that Jack made up the bed this morning. For some reason, he strikes me as the kind of guy who would leave the sheets rumpled, but they're flattened and the quilt my mom made is spread reasonably neatly over the king bed. The pillows are even fluffed.

Impressed, I head into the bathroom. As soon as I spot the soaking tub, I revise my plan to take a quick shower. I turn on the tub filler, toss in two of the peppermint-scented bath bombs from Frost & Fizz Soap Works, and pull a fluffy white towel down from the rack. Then I double check that I've locked the door to avoid any sitcom-worthy mishaps if Jack returns before I'm out of the bath.

I shed my running clothes and sink into the hot water with a contented sigh. The invigorating scent of peppermint clears my mind and I trace lazy circles in the water as my body relaxes and my brain climbs off the hamster wheel it's been on. I close my eyes and lean back, content and calm for the first time in at least twelve hours.

But as I drain the tub, my mind's already back on the kiss. No point fighting it, I need to address it—and the fallout. I step into the shower to wash my hair, and throw on jeans and a thick cable-knit sweater. It's casual for a visit to a judge, but it'll work for the tree farm later.

Judge MacIntosh's daughter Quinn answers on the second ring. By the time I wind through town to the MacIntosh's orchard near Starlight Lake, Quinn has coffee brewing and a half-dozen of Merry's cookies plated.

As soon as I walk through the door, Quinn wraps me in a tight hug and tells me to make myself comfortable before disappearing into her dad's study. I wriggle out of my coat and hang it on the rack near the door before heading into the cozy living room. I pour myself a cup of coffee and nibble on a snickerdoodle while I examine a large canvas propped against one wall. I think it's one of Pedro's but, if so, it's a departure from his signature bright colors and bold brush strokes. This abstract piece is muted, delicate, and, somehow, perfectly imperfect. I step back and consider it from a new angle.

Quinn pops her head into the room. "Dad'll be out in a minute. I wish I could stay and visit with you, but I was about to head into town to help make sets for the ballet."

I turn to smile at her. "We totally need to catch up. It's been forever since we hung out."

"I'll call you one day this week," she promises. "Lunch at Sushi Station?"

"You're on."

Judge MacIntosh appears in the doorway. Quinn gives her father a peck on the cheek before grabbing her coat and keys from the stand beside the front door. I catch the faint sound of humming and recognize "The Waltz of the Flowers" from the *Nutcracker* as she leaves.

I gesture toward the painting. "One of Pedro's?"

"Yes. He calls it *What Remains Beautiful.*"

"It's different."

He nods. "He's been experimenting with principles of wabi-sabi, finding the beauty in imperfection, impermanence, and incompleteness. Maybe you've seen cracked Japanese pottery mended with gold? It's the same idea."

A lump rises in my throat as I study the painting some

more. Art doesn't usually make me emotional, but with the judge's explanation, the clay, slate blue, and moss green geometric shapes that Pedro's painted take on new meaning. They look like ceramic shards, falling, shifting, and transforming, connected in places by a fine, golden line that suggests transition, transformation, and repair. My heart squeezes and I clear my throat. "It's evocative. Beautiful."

"I'll pass that along. He'll be glad to hear it."

"Is he in the city this weekend?" I ask the question mainly to give myself time to regain my composure.

Pedro and the judge have been together forever—at least twenty years—but Pedro has always split his time between Mistletoe Mountain and Brooklyn, where he teaches an art class and runs a gallery collective.

"Yes. He has office hours on Monday for his History of Modern Art Class, then he's coming back for the rest of the festivities. He's giving his final online this year so he doesn't miss the gingerbread house building competition."

"Well, he does have a title to defend."

"Actually, he's judging this year."

The shift in topics does its job. My emotions are tucked back into their box when Uncle Chris gestures toward the seating area. I perch on an armless chair and he settles on the low settee.

"Quinn said you need some professional advice." He pours himself a cup of coffee. "I trust it's not about the Bell case."

Ex parte communications are frowned on. We shouldn't talk about Jack's case without including someone from the district attorney's office. But I need his counsel.

"Only tangentially," I tell him. I square my shoulders and blurt it out. "I want to self-report an ethical violation."

A faint smile appears on his lips. It's so brief I think I may have imagined it. But then he says, "Ah, the kiss in the beer garden."

My jaw hinges open. "*How?* How did *you* hear about *that?*"

"Holly Evelyn Jolly," he says, "you've lived your whole life in this town. Don't you know by now that news travels through the Mistletoe Mountain grapevine faster than Santa's sleigh circles the globe?"

He has a point, but still. "You weren't even there. I didn't see Quinn either."

"You're right. I went to the social club after the tree lighting and Quinn was at a birthday party for a friend over in Stonebridge. They ended up at Rudy's with the late-night crowd. People were talking."

People were talking. I'll bet those people share my DNA. Traitorous sisters.

"So you see the problem. I kissed my client. Or he kissed me and I kissed him back." I shift my gaze to the cup in my hands unable to say "kiss" one more time to this man.

He chuckles and I lift my head. He studies me gravely over the tops of his glasses. "Things happen, Holly."

"Things happen? Things happen!" I sputter. "Tabitha and Anderson were there. He saw us."

The chuckle grows into a guffaw. "That's rich."

I stare at him. "Uncle Chris, it's not funny. Anderson threatened to report me to the bar."

He snorts and slaps his thigh. "Are you kidding? It's hilarious. Have you both forgotten who chairs the ethics committee?"

"I know it's you, that's why I'm here."

He must hear the desperate break in my voice because turns serious. "I highly doubt he's going to report you. He doesn't have the cleanest hands himself."

"That's true. I told him if he did, I'd file a complaint about him and Tabitha having an affair at the DA's office."

He nods. "Exactly. You have mutually assured destruction. I'm confident DA Waterson will stop him from making that mistake."

"I think so, too. She hustled him out of the tent in a hurry. But, just in case he goes rogue, I wanted to come to you first. I understand if you want to remove me from Jack's case."

This earns me another snort—a derisive one. "Nice try. I presume you told Mr. Bell that you can't get involved with him while you're representing him."

"I did."

"So what's the issue? You shared one kiss, Holly. If memory serves, Rule 1.8 prohibits beginning a consensual sexual relationship with a client after undertaking a representation. Presumably, I'd have heard if you and Mr. Bell had sex on the dance floor."

"Uncle Chris!"

He waves off my outburst. "Just keep it chaste for the remainder of the case. After it's wrapped up, you and Mr. Bell are free to do whatever you want."

"After it's wrapped up, he'll go back to Florida or continue on to Montreal or out West or wherever the spirit moves him," I say with a heat that surprises me. "That's not the issue."

"As far as I can tell, there is no issue."

I stare at him for a long moment. "If only the judge hadn't ordered me to live with the guy," I finally snark.

"Heh. Maybe there's one teeny issue." He finishes his coffee and rests the mug on its saucer. "In all seriousness, I'm glad you came to talk to me about it. It shows integrity."

I've clearly been dismissed, so I stand up. "Of course."

On my way out of the room, I take a final look at Pedro's painting. It hits me squarely in the feels again. "What did you say this is called?"

He follows my gaze. "*What Remains Beautiful.*"

CHAPTER 16

DANCING AROUND RULE 1.8

Jack

I'm camped out on the porch glider, my head tipped back to soak up the sun and my legs stretched out in front of me, when Holly's car pulls into the parking spot beside the cottage. As she's getting out of her car, I rise to greet her.

"Miss Jolly," I say, removing an imaginary hat from my head and sweeping it in front of me.

"Um, hi?"

I plow ahead, committed to my plan, no matter how cringe it might be. And I'm feeling like it might be *very, very* cringe. I plant myself between her and the door.

She gives me the side-eye. "Did a pile of books fall on your head while you were at the library?"

I smile but stay the course. "No. But I did read something interesting."

Her gaze darts toward the door. "Why don't you tell me about it inside—where's it warm."

"This'll only take a minute," I promise.

She sighs. "Fine. What did you read, Jack?"

"Rule 1.8(j) of *The Vermont Rules of Professional Conduct*." She blinks as I continue, "As far as I can tell, we're prohibited from having a sexual relationship while you're my lawyer."

"That's right," she chokes out, still stunned.

"But there's nothing that says we can't be friends."

"Friends?" Her eyes narrow. "Like, friends with benefits? That's definitely not allowed."

"No, like friends. Friends who are attracted to each other but aren't going to act on it—for now."

She blushes, searching my face. "That's allowed."

"Friends who might want to see what develops after the representation ends," I clarify so there's no confusion.

"What, you want me to wait for you, like you're going off to war?"

I chuckle. "Wouldn't you be the one going off to war in this analogy? But, no, I'm proposing a good old-fashioned courtship."

"Courtship? Like in an Amish romance?"

"I was thinking more along the lines of a Jane Austen novel—*Pride and Prejudice* or maybe *Emma*."

She feigns fanning herself. "Oh, Mr. Darcy, tell me more."

I shake my head. "I'm more of a Bingley. Cheerful, optimistic, prone to falling in love at first sight."

"A man who's actually read *Pride and Prejudice*," she murmurs. Then she cocks her head and eyes me from under her long lashes. "Does that make me Jane?"

"That remains to be seen. But you have a strong Lizzy vibe."

She giggles. "Well, then you're Darcy after all. But, if memory serves, Elizabeth and Darcy mainly argued."

"And danced at balls," I add. "What's that quote about dancing?"

"To be fond of dancing was a certain step towards falling in love," she supplies. "That was Charles Bingley, though. Not Darcy."

"Either way. Three holiday events a week seems like the equivalent of a season's worth of balls to me."

"Wait. Are you serious about this?"

"Completely serious," I tell her.

She leans against the banister. "What would this courtship look like?"

"It would look like us going to a dozen Christmas events and spending the rest of the time hanging out, getting to know each other. When you aren't working, of course."

"While we live together in a one-bedroom cottage."

"Alternating nights on the couch. I can behave if you

can." I say this with much more certainty than I feel. I can barely stop myself from pulling her into my arms right here, right now. But I manage to resist the impulse.

A slow smile spreads across her plump lips and her blue eyes spark. "Why not?"

"Why not," I echo as I step aside and open the door for her.

CHAPTER 17

A FOOT RUB BETWEEN FRIENDS

Holly

After a whirlwind trip to the tree farm, complete with hayride, hot mulled cider, and the annual Jolly family squabble over whether to get a shorter, full tree or a taller, more stately tree (solved, as it always is, by our dad buying one of each—one for the lobby and the other for the family room), Jack and I collapse on the small couch in the cottage's living room.

"I think my toes are frozen," I say only half-joking.

"Let's see." He gestures toward my feet.

I laugh before I look at his face. His expression is serious as he pats his jean-clad thighs. I hesitate, unsure. I've known this man for a grand total of thirty-six hours. But we're living together for the next month. And my feet *are* cold. Besides, I remind myself, the rules of conduct don't prohibit all touching. Unless he has a fetish I don't know about, there's nothing sexual about him warming up my toes. So I take a deep breath and swing my legs around. He props my feet on his thighs, peels off my thick wool socks with a gentle touch, and squeezes my bare feet.

"These are like ice cubes."

"Merry and Dad were arguing over that concolor fir for at least twenty minutes," I point out. "I should have walked around, kept my blood circulating."

He squints down at my toes. "Are your big toenails bruised?"

"Probably. Runner's toe," I explain. "I did ten miles this morning."

He lifts my feet and stands up. "Hang on."

He disappears into the bedroom and emerges a moment later holding the peppermint lotion from the bathroom vanity. When he drops back on the cushion beside me, I return my cold, tired feet to his lap. Then I lean back and close my eyes while he massages the thick, scented lotion into my heels, soles, and each individual toe with strong, warm fingers.

I melt into the couch, as relaxed as I've ever been. So relaxed, in fact, that I drift off to sleep.

When I awake I do so gently, my senses coming back online gradually. I feel the caress of the light blanket that's been draped over me, smell the zing of mint from the lotion that's melted into my feet, and hear the gentle pop and crackle of burning wood. There's another sound, too, the whisper of turning pages.

I push myself up on my elbows and scan the dim room. The light from the flames dancing in the fireplace reflects in the lighted garland that graces the mantel and the glass bowl filled with silver balls that sits atop it. At last, my gaze lands on Jack. He's draped sideways across the striped chair by the window, his legs dangling over one arm of the chair and his head bent over a book. The last rays of sunset wash over his profile, lighting his cheekbones and the wave of sandy hair that falls over his forehead.

My heart doesn't just flutter at the sight—it does the full dance of the sugarplum fairy in my chest. The moment feels profoundly intimate and utterly innocent at the same time. I watch his brow furrow in concentration as he reads, follow the arc of his thumb absently tracing the edge of the page. The memory of those same hands massaging my bare feet sends a rush of blood to my face.

He must feel the weight of my gaze because he lifts his head and catches me gaping at him.

"Good nap?"

"The best," I purr as I stretch.

I glance at the clock in the kitchen and reach for my socks. "We should get over to the main house if we want to help trim the trees."

"What about dinner?" He sticks a bookmark between the pages and closes the cover.

"There'll be heavy hors d'oeuvres and drinks in the

lobby," I tell him. "Then dessert and coffee or hot cocoa while we decorate the family tree. Believe me, you won't go hungry."

While he douses the fire, I hurry to the bathroom to drag a brush through my wind-tangled and sleep-smooshed hair.

When we step out onto the porch, I shiver. What little warmth the day held is seeping away with the setting sun. I'm about to turn back for a hat and a warmer coat, but he's already unwrapping the thick maroon scarf from around his neck. He loops it over my shoulders and around my nose, leaving the fringed ends hanging down my back.

"Thanks," I say, my voice muffled under the fabric.

"Don't mention it. It's what any member of the Regency landed gentry would do."

He smirks, and I smile into his pine- and sandalwood-scented scarf. I could get used to this courtship business.

CHAPTER 18

A PURPLE FINCH IN A SPRUCE TREE

Jack

Holly is either blissfully unaware of the effect she has on me or a hard-core sadist. Given that much of the effect in question happened *while she was sleeping*, I'm going with the former. I resorted to plucking a random book from the stack by the chair to distract myself from her pink cheeks and little sleep sighs while she napped on the couch.

By a cruel quirk of fate, the book I chose was none other than *Before the Storm Breaks*, a prequel novel to the Jackie Samuel's Resistance series Noelle was gushing over at the library. In fact, this particular book is so niche it's never appeared on the banned and challenged books list, unlike the rest of the series. I almost put it down and chose another title. But it's been a good five years, maybe longer, since I read any of the books in the series and, weird as this sounds, I thought perhaps fate led me to pick it up.

And by the time I was forty pages in, I knew I was right. The prose took me back to a past Jack. Teenaged Jack, with all his questioning, raging, and flailing. Early twenties Jack, with all his screwups, false starts, and failures. But as they always did, the characters reassured me that I'd find the light, carve a path, do the thing. While it remains an open question whether I've done that, the book, man, it didn't disappoint. By the time Holly's adorable sleep sounds faded and she stirred, I was just two chapters from the end and had to blink away tears before I looked up at her.

Reading the book did two things: it successfully kept me from violating the courtship rules the same day we agreed to them, and it reminded me why I'm on this banned book crusade in the first place. People—kids, yes, but big people, too—need stories like these. Stories that challenge them. Sad, even tragic, stories. Stories about characters on the margins. When I look at it through this lens, even the threat of jail time doesn't dissuade me. Screw Anderson Wilson Carson and screw Citizens Upholding Normal Traditions.

As Holly and I cross the frozen path from the little cottage to the inn, my mind is on the books. I can hardly wait to put my head together with Noelle and plan the holiday banned book bingo. I'm lost in thought when Holly gasps and clutches my arm.

I turn. She's pointing toward a small rose-pink bird

with dark gray tail feathers perched on a limb of one of the snow-covered spruce trees lining the walking path. It turns its bright black eyes toward us.

"It's a purple finch," she whispers.

"It's not purple," I whisper back.

She laughs. "I know. Poor thing has been misnamed. Merry used call them raspberry birds."

"That's more fitting."

"They were one of my mom's favorite signs of Christmas. I haven't seen one since she …"

I wait a moment, but she doesn't go on. I clear my throat. "We have a bird called the red junglefowl in the Keys. They look kind of like dressed-up roosters."

She raises an eyebrow and coughs out a laugh, so I keep talking. "They do. They have brilliant red combs, golden breast feathers, and bright emerald bodies with these majestic onyx black tail feathers. Anyway, one December, when money was tight, we woke up to see an army of these things in our backyard. My mom told me and my brother they were partridges looking for a pear tree. That year, our gifts were all things from the song, and Sam and I thought the 'partridges' had come there especially for us."

I chuckle at the memory, and she smiles up at me. "Your mom must have had a vivid imagination."

"You have no idea," I tell her.

There's one fat tear shining on her cheek. I take off my glove and wipe it away. Her breath catches in her throat and she stares at me, her lips parting. I lean forward. Then she shakes her head and croaks, "Rule 1.8."

I exhale in a loud whoosh that earns me a scolding from the purple finch. Then I swallow. "Right. Rule 1.8."

Holly rallies first.

"Come on," she grabs my bare hand and drags me toward the house. "I'm starving. Let's get some appetizers."

This is going to be a long, long month.

CHAPTER 19

A FUNERAL WOULD BE MORE FUN

Holly

Monday morning rolls around entirely too soon for my taste. I wake up on the couch, unwind my cramped limbs, and crack my back. I pad into the kitchen in the fuzzy slipper socks I stole from Noelle, start the coffeemaker, and open the refrigerator.

After the tree-trimming extravaganza on Saturday, Noelle and Dad sent us home with two giant bags full of neatly packaged leftovers and two wholly unnecessary bottles of wine. The wine is stashed in the wine fridge built into the island and the food, along with Merry's desserts, fills the refrigerator. Unfortunately, none of it screams "healthy breakfast."

We could have, should have, gone to the market yesterday, but we spent our Sunday in our pajamas, lazing in front of the fire and reading. It was a reasonable approximation of how I planned to spend my solo anti-Christmas month—with the notable addition of Jack.

The coffee finishes brewing and I pour myself a mug. After a moment, I pull down a second mug and pour Jack one, too. Even though it pains me, I paw through the fridge until I find the bottle of eggnog-flavored creamer that Noelle slipped with the leftovers and splash a healthy dollop into Jack's mug. Then I cross the living room, shifting the second mug from my left hand to my right, and rap on the bedroom door.

"Hrmph." He sounds like a bear. Or maybe a Yeti.

"Are you decent?" I call. "I have caffeine."

"Give me a second," he responds in a more human-sounding voice.

I listen to the rustling through the door and can't stop myself from wondering if he sleeps naked. Thankfully, before my thoughts wander too far down this path, the door swings open. Jack stands in the doorway, blinking. His hair is a shock of thick honey sticking straight up. His smooth chest is bare, but, praise Santa, he's wearing a pair of buffalo plaid fleece pajama bottoms.

"Here." I thrust the sweetened coffee toward him.

"Uh, thanks." He takes it and gives me a bemused, sleepy smile.

Before he can close the door and shuffle back to bed, I step over the threshold. He opens his eyes wider. I laugh and put a hand on his chest, then realize what I've done and pull my hand back like he's a hot stove.

"Sorry. I know you don't have anywhere to be this morning, but I kind of need to use the bathroom and get ready for work." I glance at the alarm clock by the bedside and add apologetically, "Nowish."

Understanding dawns on his face and he scrubs a hand over his beard. "Right. Of course."

He shuffles out into the living room, clutching the coffee between his hands, and I make a beeline for the bathroom.

When I emerge thirty minutes later, I look like Lawyer Holly. I'm wearing a black sheath dress with white piping and matching suit jacket, a pair of low-heeled pumps, and a strand of pearls. I've tamed my hair into a sleek bun and applied minimal makeup. Jack, still shirtless, lounges on the couch with his coffee and a sticky bun.

"Are you going to a funeral?" he asks around a mouthful of cinnamon dough.

"So close. I have a meeting at the DA's office."

He swallows. "About my case?"

I gulp down my last mouthful of room-temperature coffee. "Yep."

His feet hit the floor as he straightens. "Should I come?"

I shake my head and walk into the kitchen to fill my travel mug with more coffee. "No need. This is just a preliminary meeting to hammer out discovery issues. You should do something less boring. Do you have any plans?"

He joins me at the counter, and the kitchen suddenly feels extremely close, cramped, and crowded. Probably because his bare chest is three, maybe four, inches away from my face. He reaches across me for the coffee carafe. I wheel around and yank the refrigerator door open. I plunk the creamer down on the counter near his mug and take a giant step backward like we're playing a silent game of Mother, May I.

"I'm going to work on the banned booked bingo with a committee from the library over lunch. But aside from that the only thing on my schedule is our first Christmas event."

He says this in a deliberately casual tone.

"What event?" I squeak.

He walks past me, brushing my arm with his, and points to the calendar I stuck to the freezer door with a whimsical snowman magnet. "Christmas Karaoke at the Tipsy Turnip." He taps today's block with his finger for emphasis.

"Christmas karaoke?" I bleat.

"Sure. It sounds like a blast. Besides, I heard you singing while we were decorating the tree."

My cheeks flame. "The family tree. In private. I don't sing in public."

He cocks his head and studies my face. "Why not?"

"Because I'm not good enough to sing in front of people. I'll make a fool of myself."

"It's karaoke, Holly. Nobody expects a professional performance."

But *I* do. What's the point of doing something poorly? What does that accomplish? Other than humiliating myself and undermining my credibility, of course. While Jack waits patiently for me to explain my reluctance, I'm reminded of Pedro's painting. What had the judge said? Wabi-sabi celebrates the beauty in the imperfect and broken. Something along those lines.

I fill my lungs with air and exhale slowly, almost disbelieving the words I hear come from my own lips. "Okay, sure. Why not?"

He grins a thousand-watt smile that warms my whole body. "Bells, yeah!"

"Did you just say … bells, yeah?"

His mouth twitches. "Keep workshopping that one?"

"Uh, yeah." I screw the lid on my travel mug and grab my coat. "One more thing, I have one condition for karaoke." I lean in and give him a serious look. "Tell no one."

The day crawls by. Whenever I have an appointment in the afternoon—whether it's something I'm looking forward to or, as in this case, something I'm heartily dreading—time seems to slow down and drag. Given the option, I'll always schedule meetings for first thing in the morning. Because Anderson knows this, I assume the two o'clock time for our meet and confer at his office is an intentional power play. I resolve not to let him get in my head but find it nearly impossible to concentrate.

This is how I end up running "Jack Bell," "Jack Bell Florida Keys," "Jack Bell Sam Bell," "Jack Bell nomad," and, finally, "Jack Bell witness protection" through every public and private search engine the public defender's office has access to. The fact that my searches turn up nothing does distract me from the impending showdown—er, negotiation—with Anderson, but not in the way I'd hoped.

Who *is* this guy? And why is he a cipher?

Ruminating over these two questions consumes my afternoon until it's time to leave for my meeting. But once I walk into the district attorney's office, I put Jack's nonexistent internet footprint out of my mind. I'm battle-ready when I present myself at the reception desk.

"Hi, Chantal."

She gives me a knowing smile. "Hey, Holly. Twice in two workdays. Lucky us, and unlucky you." Her voice drops. "They're ready for you in Conference Room B."

"Thanks. Wait—they?"

Her right eyebrow twitches upward. "Tabitha is sitting in. She had me move a conference call."

I take a beat to process this news. My initial reaction is that being double-teamed by the DA dream team is a blow, but once I think it through, I realize there's exactly one person who will be less pleased than I am by the district attorney's involvement in this case. And that person is

Anderson Wilson Carson, Esquire. My day just improved by about one million percent.

"Hello," I chirp as I walk into the conference room.

"Holly." Anderson pops to his feet, trying and failing to hide his sour expression.

Tabitha stays seated but extends her hand.

I ignore him and reach across the table to shake her hand, then pull out a seat and snap open my briefcase. Anderson drops back into his chair.

I make two decisions: one, to take charge of this meeting and, two, to address Tabitha rather than Anderson as much as possible. It's an appropriate course of action— she is the chief DA, after all. The fact that it'll leave Anderson silently seething is simply gravy, thick, delicious gravy.

"To begin," I say, focusing exclusively on Tabitha, "I'd like to schedule Vicky Swanson's deposition as soon as possible."

Tabitha holds my gaze. "Before we start scheduling discovery, you should know that there's been some outside interest in this case."

Neither of us so much as glances at Anderson, but her tone leaves no doubt that she's displeased with him.

"What kind of outside interest?"

"Vicky's hung up flyers advertising a public meeting to discuss the books she deems inappropriate. She's apparently planning to form a group."

I nod. Noelle told me about this. "I've heard. Her choice

of name for the organization is ...unfortunate." I want to say classic, hilarious, or over-the-top, but I keep my composure.

Tabitha chokes back a laugh. "Yes, well. Thanks to its name, her flyers announcing Citizens Upholding Normal Traditions went viral on social media."

"How viral?"

"Think pandemic viral. Kids are stitching the image, creating songs, sharing it everywhere."

A giggle escapes me. I can't help it.

"The problem for your client and my office is that it caught the attention of a well-financed, nationwide coalition of book banners, either as a result of all the social media posts or through some other channel." She pauses to shoot Anderson a displeased, somewhat distrustful look. "However they learned about, they're about to descend on the town during the height of the holiday season—with the media in tow. It's not ideal."

I shoot a glance at Anderson, who can't manage to hide his smug grin.

"It's not ideal for most of us," I agree. "Anyone with political ambitions is probably thrilled, though."

This observation wipes the grin off his face. I don't stop to wonder if he shared his five-year plan with Tabitha because I frankly don't care. Because I know him. He'll use the publicity to advance his career any way he can, no matter who he hurts in the process.

"This is an important issue," he interjects. "Communities all around the country are dealing with it. We have the opportunity to contribute to the conversation in a meaningful way."

"Spare me. The only contribution this case will make is as a textbook example of prosecutorial overreach." I turn my attention back to Tabitha. "Do I need to ask Judge MacIntosh for a gag order?"

"I've instructed my staff and the Swansons not to comment publicly on the case. So I don't think a gag order is necessary."

I shift my gaze back to my ex-fiancé. "Bet that stings, huh, Anderson?"

His nostrils flare. "I have told you I go by Anders now. It's disrespectful not use my preferred name and—"

"You're right. It is. And ordinarily, I would respect someone's preferences. But when that *someone* disrespected me by having sex in a closet with our boss six months before our planned wedding, they're not entitled to my respect. You're lucky I don't call you something much worse than your stupid given name."

I close my briefcase. "I take it we're not scheduling discovery today?" Even though my heart is thumping, my voice is steady as I address Tabitha.

"No. I wanted to give you a head's up about the media," she says. Then she holds my gaze. "About the other thing …"

I wait. She shakes her head and finally says, "I'm sorry it happened the way it did."

I stand up and walk out without another word. Tabitha's apology rings hollow. It's far too little, far too late. But she's right—the way it happened was worse than necessary. Not that there's a good way to discover your fiancé's true character.

Although maybe if I'd been honest with myself earlier and admitted that every compromise I made to keep the peace chipped away at who I was, I would have been able to walk away with my dignity intact. Instead, I was so opposed to admitting I made a mistake that I let Anderson shape me into his ideal district attorney's wife until I was nothing but a shell wearing pearls and drinking wine spritzers.

I take a steadying breath as I push through the heavy door into the stairwell so I can go out the back way and avoid Chantal's scrutiny. Looking back, all the signs were there—as obvious as blinking Christmas lights. I just closed my eyes to them.

CHAPTER 20

THE FIRST OFFICIAL CHRISTMAS NON-DATE

Jack

I'm beginning to think Holly won't show. If she stands me up, I'll not only be embarrassed, I'll also be in violation of a court order, so I really, really hope I'm wrong. As I'm about to check my watch for the seventh time, the door to the Tipsy Turnip blows open and she hurries inside in a whirl of blonde curls and red feathers. She's freed her hair from the bun and, while she's still wearing her suit dress, she's traded the jacket for a festive, flowy, fuzzy wrap that floats along behind her. She looks like a scarlet tanager, the migratory red and black song-bird, as she stands in the doorway and scans the room. I grin at the image then wave my hand to catch her attention.

She winds her way through the crowd to join us at the

long, gleaming black table Delphina saved for our group right near the karaoke stage. She locks eyes with me unblinkingly as she approaches. I pat the empty metal stool next to mine and she slides onto it.

She places her mouth close to my ear. "What part of 'tell no one' confused you?"

I rear back and meet her eyes. "I thought you said 'tell Noelle!'"

Her irritation dissolves and she throws back her head and laughs. "That explains the crowd."

Merry, Ivy, a woman named Quinn, some guy named Enzo, and Delphina and Titus are crowded around our table. Nick gives Holly a wave from the next table over, where he sits with Noelle, Griselda, a lawyer named Marley, Josh and Ryan Morgenthal, and a retired teacher named Enrique. At least, I think those are their names—the introductions were brief and shouted over the din.

A server swings by with a stack of coasters and a wide, genuine smile. "I see a new face. So, here's the skinny— we're a farm to table restaurant. Chase owns the farm and the restaurant. His partner Amelia pairs the cocktails and wines with our menu. Tonight, it's a limited pairing in honor of Christmas karaoke. Any questions?"

Holly scans the table, sees a sea of shaking heads, then gestures for the menus. "We're in Chase's hands—and Amelia's. Thanks, Rory." She takes the menus and hands them over.

Rory takes them with a nod. "Excellent decision."

The server leaves and Holly turns to her sisters. "So what are we singing?"

Ivy grimaces and elbows Merry. Merry throws a desperate look at Quinn, who shakes her head. Finally, Delphina bravely steps into the breach.

"Holls, you were late. And you know how fast signups go. So, the four of us are singing together." She gestures toward the other three women. "But Jack signed the two of you up for a duet. Talk to him. Kaythanxbye."

Holly gives her best friend a death stare for several seconds before turning to me. "I'm afraid to ask."

"Merry Christmas, Baby."

"Uh. Merry Christmas to you, too. What are we singing?"

I chuckle. "No, that's what we're singing. 'Merry Christmas, Baby,' the Colbie Caillat and Brad Paisley version."

"I don't know this song." Panic crosses her face.

I pull it up on my phone and hand it to her. "I'm sure you do."

She takes the phone and studies it like it holds the nuclear codes. I put my hand over hers. "It's karaoke, Holly. The stakes literally couldn't be lower."

For a long moment, she looks at me like I'm speaking Portuguese. Then she nods. Shrugs. Exhales. "Right. Who cares?"

"Exactly."

She stands up. "Excuse me."

"You're not going to bolt, are you?" I joke.

"No, of course not. I'm going to the ladies' room to warm up my vocal cords," she says in a tone that suggests this is the most obvious answer imaginable.

So much for low-stakes karaoke.

She returns at the same time Rory arrives at the table with a tray laden with bright red drinks. "These are mocktails," Rory says. "A refreshing combo of soda water with a splash of cranberry and a twist of lime. Despite our name, the Tipsy Turnip is all for pacing yourself."

There's a small wave of appreciative laughter from the table that fades when a Black woman wearing a Santa hat and a nose ring steps up to the low stage. She switches on the microphone and says, "Hey, ho, here we go! I'm DJ Nebula and Christmas Karaoke is *on*." She checks her list. "First up, we have The Not-So Mean Girls, Delph, Quinn, Ivy, and Merry, performing 'Jingle Bell Rock.'"

They leave the table in a flurry of laughter and take the stage. Someone from the other side of the room calls out, "Do 'Santa Baby!'" Merry flips a good-natured bird in the general direction of the shout as the music begins.

The four do a high-energy, mostly in-tune rendition of the song and flop back into their seats to a chorus of clapping and *woos* from the crowd—the loudest applause coming from their dad's table. Holly leans across me to tell them how fabulous they were and I catch a whiff of something citrusy and spicy. Her shampoo? Perfume? Whatever it is, it's dizzying. I grab my glass and gulp the drink to keep myself from reaching for her.

The DJ calls Marley and Griselda to the stage. They're physical opposites: the tall, sinewy, severe-looking fitness instructor and the petite, curvy lawyer. But once they begin to sing, they're anything but an odd pair. They perform a hot, sultry take on "Baby, It's Cold Outside" that's somehow raw emotion and polished professionalism at the same time.

Delphina leans across the table to whisper to Holly, "Are they together?"

Holly whispers back, "I don't know, but if they're not, they should be."

The women finish their song to a standing ovation that seems to go on forever. Griselda grins and curtseys while Marley appears to be dazed.

When they leave the stage, DJ Nebula is still clapping. She glances at her list. "Whew, Nick and Noelle, you have a hard act to follow."

Nick bounds up to the stage after stopping to hug the two women headed back to their seats. Noelle lags behind but eventually joins him with a shy smile. She looks at the DJ and says, "Okay, we're ready." Nebula hits the music and Nick and Noelle launch into "Every Day Is Christmas." They're no Marley and Griselda, but their joy's infectious. Nick's daughters all wear expressions that convey how thrilled and grateful they are that their father's found love again with Noelle. I feel a pang for my mom, that she never truly had that.

But the ache disappears, swallowed by my helpless

laughter, during Ryan Morgenthal's hilarious rendition of Adam Sandler's "The Hanukkah Song." Josh stomps his feet and whistles through his fingers.

Small plates of olive crackers and goat cheese arrive, paired with crisp white wine. I've got a mouthful of both when I hear my name and Holly's being called. I hurry to wash the bite down with some wine, stand, and hold out my hand to her. "Are you ready?"

"Not even remotely," she says, dabbing at her mouth with her napkin. But she hops off the stool and slips her hand into mine. Her skin is cool and I feel a slight tremble in her hand. I give it as reassuring squeeze as we climb the stairs to the stage.

The song starts, and my gaze shifts between the lyrics on the screen and Holly, standing with her body angled toward me. Luckily, my choice of song has remarkably few lyrics. It's mostly the repeated refrain that we say back and forth to each other. She keeps her focus on me the entire time, like I'm her lifeline.

By the time the song nears the end, she's relaxed enough to close her eyes and belt out the chorus. We finish and she flashes me a smile that could light the entire town square's holiday displays.

We leave the stage with a wave as a burst of applause rises. As we reach the floor, she leans into me to say, "That was fun. I'm glad we did it."

My hands find her upper arms, and I stare into her clear bright, blue eyes. "So am I."

She holds my gaze, and her tongue darts out to wet her lips before she clears her throat. "And it's exactly the sort of thing that will make people feel warmly toward you at trial. So it was a great strategic idea."

I study her. I can't tell if she's being lawyerly because it's her default state or if she's doing it to put distance between herself and the moment of crackling intensity that passed between us. So I just nod, unable to say anything around the sudden tightness in my throat. I remind myself it doesn't matter—we're constrained from acting on anything we might be feeling, anyway. But that doesn't take away the question.

A COWARDLY FEAR OF KNOWLEDGE

Holly

I hum "Merry Christmas, Baby" to myself at my desk while I read a stack of cases involving unlawful trespass under Section 3705(c). To my complete lack of surprise, not a single case involves a box. I'm in my work groove, lost in concentration. So when my phone chirps, it takes me a moment to register that I have a call and another beat to realize it's my cell phone, not my work line.

I dig my phone out of my briefcase and glance at the display, seeing that it's Noelle.

"Hello?" I manage to pick up the call just before it rolls to voicemail.

"Holly, can you hear me?"

"Barely." Her voice is nearly drowned out by loud, sustained shouting in the background. "Where are you?"

"I'm at the library. Hold on, I'll go back inside." The noise fades. "Better?"

"Yes. What is that racket? It sounds like someone chanting."

"It is. That's why I'm calling. There was a small group of protesters outside the building when I got here. They've grown since then."

"Protesters?" I echo dumbly.

"Yeah, I think they're here to support Vicky's book ban plans, based on their signs and slogans. They're from out of town, I think. I don't recognize any of them and the library lot is full of cars with out-of-state plates."

Tabitha's prediction is coming true already, I think.

"How many are there?" I ask.

"Several dozen, now. They're blocking the entrance and the kids can't get in for story time. Here, I'll send you a video."

There's a pause, then my email notification dings. I open the attachment she just sent and watch the recording on my laptop. A large group of people march in front of the library, waving signs that read "Protect Our Children," "No Dirty Books," and "Keep Filth Out." They shout indistinctly as they picket the entrance.

"Did you get it?" Noelle asks, her tone low and urgent.

"Yeah, I'm watching it now." The protestors' faces are red and angry as spittle flies from their open, screaming mouths. On the screen Clem and Brent Stillwater appear in the frame, headed toward the doors. Clem stops, scoops up his grandson, and heads for the back of the building. The shouting continues. My stomach clenches, and I pause the video. I've seen enough.

"Did Clem bring Brent through the back entrance?"

"Yes, and after I let them in, I locked the doors. Holly, I don't know what to do. I don't want these protestors coming inside, but the library is a public place." Her voice shakes.

I take a deep breath. I have to keep it together so I can help her stay calm.

"Here's what we're going to do. I'll contact Judge MacIntosh's chambers and explain what's happening. Yes, these people have a right to protest, but they can't block public access to the library—or the sidewalk for that matter. I'll get an emergency order and come over to deal with them. You stay inside. Don't confront the protestors. Call the county police and ask them to send someone to maintain order. I'll be there as soon as I can."

The relief in her voice is palpable when she thanks me.

I hang up and type furiously, my fingers flying over the keys, as I draft the emergency order. As far as I know, this group doesn't have a formal connection to the case against Jack. So I feel no compulsion to give the district attorney's office a head's up.

Instead, I dial Judge MacIntosh's chambers and quickly explain the situation to Roz. Then I email her the order and wait for her to call me back. I'm too keyed up to work.

For some reason, the first person I think to call is Jack. I don't stop to question this impulse. Instead, I try his cellphone. The call goes to voicemail and I hang up without leaving a message. I resort to drumming my fingers on my desk.

As soon the phone starts to ring, I snatch it up. "H. Evelyn Jolly."

Roz's speech is rapid fire. "The judge just signed the order. If you swing by to pick it up, I'll meet you down in the lobby."

"I'm on my way," I say, grabbing my keys and coat.

By the time I get the order from Roz and drive over to the library, the crowd has swelled to over a hundred people. Where are they even coming from? The entire town is booked solid with Christmas tourists. They have to be staying somewhere else. I drive past the library at a crawl and park in the alley behind Ivy and Merry's place on Poinsettia Way. Then I sprint back to the library, praying I don't slip on a patch of ice as I dodge groups of shoppers and an elf passing out candy canes near the jewelry store.

When I skid to a stop at the corner of the library, I spot Jack standing on the low retaining wall along the front of the building. His arms are crossed, his face tense, as he stares down the protesters. I pull out my phone and call Noelle.

"I have the order," I pant. "Meet me in the parking lot."

I round the building and arrive in the lot as she's slipping out the back door. Behind her, Farah locks the door from the inside.

Noelle's face is pale, her freckles prominent against her skin. But her green eyes blaze. "What's the plan?"

"I'm going to serve them with the order. We'll ask the police to help move them across the street."

"The green space with the fountain and the benches?"

I nod. "It's safer for them, and everyone else."

She grabs my hand. "Thank you."

We lock elbows and walk arm-in-arm around the side of the building. Then we squeeze up on the steps in front of the entrance to put ourselves between the library and the protesters. Jack swivels his head toward us. His eyes bore into me with a fierce promise to keep us safe.

My heart falters at the unspoken vow and my breath catches. I try to smile. I'm sure it looks more like a grimace.

"Who's in charge here?" Noelle calls, her voice loud and clear, while I grip the railing and steady my emotions.

A man with close-cropped gray hair, wearing a leather bomber jacket that's nowhere near warm enough for a Vermont winter, steps forward. "I am. James Woodlock. I lead the coalition of groups that organize under the national umbrella of Clean Books, Healthy Minds."

I raise an eyebrow at the moniker but keep my expression neutral. Defusion is the name of this game.

"I'm Noelle Winters, director of this library, and this is our attorney, H. Evelyn Jolly."

I take over. "The library welcomes community input. And though you folks don't seem to be local, we recognize your group's right to protest. But you can't block public access to the library or the sidewalk. By order of court, you'll need to move to the fountain courtyard across the street." I gesture toward the space.

Woodlock starts to grumble, and I hand him the order. "It's a matter of local ordinance," I explain. "The county police will be happy to escort your group safely across the street." I point behind me to Liza and Ned, who flank the front doors with their hands on their holsters.

The protesters behind him start up a chant, but he raises a hand to cut them off. They fall silent as he scowls down at Judge MacIntosh's order. Then he looks up, casting a glare directly at Jack, who meets it with a hard look of his own. They lock eyes for a long moment, before Woodlock looks away.

He folds the order in half, sticks it in his jacket pocket, and turns to address his group. "A court order's a court order. Let's go."

Ned and Liza stop traffic to let them stream across High Street to the courtyard, tramping through the slushy snow.

Noelle wraps me in a tight hug. "Thank you."

I exhale, relieved Woodlock acquiesced without a fight,

but I can't relax. "I don't think it's over yet. In fact, I'm pretty sure it's just getting started."

"I know, but at least the kids can get inside now. That's the important thing." She gives me a wan smile and walks inside.

Jack strolls over to join me on the steps and gives me an appraising look. "You handled them well. These folks aren't usually so reasonable."

"How do you know them?" I ask, curious.

"What do you mean?"

"That Woodlock guy—the look you gave each other. It seems like there's a history there."

He shakes his head and his shoulders tense. "It doesn't matter."

It matters to me. If he has a connection to these protesters, I need to know what it is in case it affects my defense. And, if I'm being honest, the evasion stings on a personal level, too. But before I can press him, Farah emerges from the library.

"Shouldn't you be at school?" I say.

She waves a hand. "I'm doing a work experience this semester with Noelle. I have an idea to run by you. I could get my AP Literature class to stage a counter-protest where we read excerpts from banned books from the library steps. Would that cause problems? Noelle wanted me to ask you."

I study the steps. "It's a brilliant idea. Just make sure your group doesn't block the entrance."

"We can sit on the wall," she points to the brick retaining wall where Jack had just been standing, "and get up one at a time to read."

I give her a grin. "Perfect. It's brave of you to organize this, Farah."

She shakes her head. "No. It's cowardly of them to fear knowledge."

She looks at the group across the street for a long moment before she turns and marches back into the library with a determined gleam in her eye.

Jack and I watch her go.

"These fools picked the wrong small town to mess with this time," he muses.

I glance across the street at the protesters, then back at Farah through the library window as she gestures animatedly while talking to Noelle. Maybe Jack's right.

CHAPTER 22

A COMMUNITY CONVERSATION

Jack

After Woodlock and his merry band of banners showed up at the library yesterday, I knew I couldn't miss Vicky Swanson's community meeting tonight. I wanted to let Holly know I plan to attend, but I haven't seen her since our conversation on the library steps. She worked into the wee hours last night and was already gone when I woke up on the loveseat this morning. I know she came home because there was a fresh pot of coffee when I woke up. But it was the only evidence she'd been there.

As I hurry down High Street, I pull out my phone to shoot her a quick text. Before I get the chance, I hear my name. I turn around to see Delphina and Quinn jogging behind me. They neatly avoid colliding with a dog walker who holds three leashes in each hand. All six pooches wear reindeer antlers and red sweaters. They also, shockingly, don't react to two women zooming past them. I'm still marveling at the dog whisperer when Quinn and Delphina reach me.

"Going to the library?" Quinn guesses.

"I am. Are you? I didn't think the Citizens Upholding Normal Traditions meeting for concerned residents would be a big draw."

Delphina laughs. "That's because you don't know Mistletoe Mountain."

Despite her cheerful tone, this proclamation puts me on edge. Is the town going to be receptive to Woodlock's spiel? Walking into the packed library meeting room does nothing to ease my concerns.

Every seat is filled and we squeeze into the line of people standing shoulder to shoulder along the back wall. My best friends from the county police force are present for crowd control. Officer Ned stands in the front right behind Anderson Carson, who's shaking hands with a woman who can only be a local television reporter, judging by her full face of makeup and the guy following her around with a camera on his shoulder. The front row is filled with faces I recognize as members of Clean Books, Healthy Minds. The only person I can't place is the slight dark-haired woman wearing slacks and a bright red turtle-neck sweater. She sits in the middle of them holding a "Citizens Upholding Normal Traditions" sign on a wooden stick.

I tap Delphina and gesture toward the woman. "Is that Vicky Swanson?"

She snickers. "Yeah, nice of her to self-identify as a—ow!"

Quinn gives her a sharp elbow to the ribs. "Be nice. Remember?"

"I remember," Delphina pouts.

"Remember what?" I ask.

"Holly made us all promise to take the high road tonight. No matter what."

Who's all, I wonder? Then I study the sea of people more closely. Although the seats in front have been claimed by Woodlock and his followers, there are a lot of folks from town in this room, and I realize most of them are wearing white. I turn back to Quinn and Delphina and notice they're both sporting snowy white sweaters.

"Did I not a get a memo?" I ask, gesturing toward my blue shirt.

"Apparently not," Quinn grins.

Before I can pursue the subject, Holly races into the room. She blinks and comes to a stop when she spots me.

"Jack, I didn't expect to see you here." She lowers her voice. "This meeting isn't directly related to the case against you, but I need you to promise not to speak up."

I nod. "Got it."

She gives me a knowing look. "Promise."

"Fine. I promise."

I hold her gaze until Anderson sniffs from the front of the room. "Counselor, we're all waiting for you."

Her smile tightens as she walks up the aisle to sit next to Noelle. Noelle wears a white sweater dress, Holly, a white pantsuit. Yeah, this was definitely coordinated. I lean against the wall and wonder what else they have up their sleeves.

Anderson raises his hands like a preacher at the pulpit and the chatter dies. "Most of you probably know me, but for those who don't, I'm Assistant District Attorney Anders Carson. Thank you all for coming out tonight. It's heartening to see such a strong turnout for this important community meeting. Especially during this busy time of year. So I'll turn this over to Mrs. Swanson so we don't keep you away from your holiday celebrations any longer than necessary."

Vicky Swanson starts to rise, but Holly steps up to the microphone. "Before we hear from Mrs. Swanson, I want to say something in my role as counsel to the library. This is a *community* meeting. While we welcome interested spectators from outside Mistletoe Mountain, only residents of the town will be permitted to speak." She looks James Woodlock dead in the eye and holds up a stack of papers. "The post office provided a list of every name and address in our zip code. If you aren't on this list, we will not be hearing from you this evening."

A rumble of complaint ripples through the protesters.

Officer Ned takes a step forward. "Anyone who disagrees is welcome to leave."

The crowd quiets and I shake my head in admiration. Woodlock 0, Holly 1.

Holly gestures toward Vicky. "You've got the floor, Mrs. Swanson."

The older woman walks to the microphone stand still clutching her sign. She stands, ill at ease, and scans the room. Her gaze falls on Woodlock and she seems to gather her thoughts.

"Hello. I'm Victoria Swanson." She glances toward Holly and says, "I live at 128 Lake Road." She waits for Holly to nod before going on. "I called this meeting because it came to my attention that some of the books that were placed in my little free library without my permission last week are unsavory. Now, I called the police because there was a strange man lurking in my yard, but once the district attorney explained what *kind* of materials had been added to my library, well, I knew it was a bigger issue. It impacts the whole town."

Holly turns and gives Anderson a look that could freeze water. He looks away fast.

Noelle leans forward. "Mrs. Swanson, are you saying Mr. Carson told you the books had been banned in other towns?"

"That's exactly what I'm saying. I didn't know. Now,

Ms. Winters, you know how I feel about some of the inappropriate books that I see on the library shelves. Witchcraft, bad language, sex." She says this last word in a hush. "But these books in my box, they're even worse."

Noelle waits a beat. "Are you finished?"

Vicky looks like she's not sure. She shifts her gaze to Woodlock, who makes a 'more' motion. "Um, I just think we, as a community, need to commit to wholesome literature. For the children. Thank you."

She hurries back to her seat, red-faced.

Noelle rises. "As the library director, I could spend the next hour telling you why Mrs. Swanson's view is so dangerous and harmful to the children. But maybe it would be better to hear it from them." She holds up a copy of the graphic novel, *Persepolis*. "This is one of the books in question."

Farah edges her way to the front of the room and stands in front of the microphone. "I'm Farah Abboud. I'm a senior at the high school, and I work here part-time at the library. I'm going to college on a full scholarship next year. *Persepolis* was my favorite book when I was in middle school. It was actually a series, but I read them all in a collection. It was the first time I read a book about a girl like me." She fingers her hijab absently. "And the courage the characters showed in the face of the Iranian Revolution, especially Marji, gave me the courage to try new things and accept who I am."

She looks directly at Vicky Swanson for a moment before she steps away from the microphone.

"Thank you, Farah." Noelle holds up copies of *Mommy, Mama, and Me* and *Charlotte's Web*. "Now, we're going to hear from Sunny Min and Brent Stillwater." She gives an encouraging smile, and Farah ushers the little girl who flipped the switch to light the tree on Friday night and the chess-playing ringer from the children's wing to the front of the room. The kids hold hands tightly.

Noelle removes the mic from the stand and crouches beside them. "Who wants to go first?"

"I will," Sunny says. She leans forward and takes the copy of *Mommy, Mama, and Me* in her hands. "When I was little, I loved this picture book." She pauses as soft laughter floats through the room at her phrasing. Noelle gives her an encouraging smile. "I loved it because it showed a family like mine. It would make me sad if other little kids didn't get to see pictures of families like theirs."

"Thank you, Sunny," Noelle says.

"Your turn, Brent," Sunny says. "You got this."

There's another chuckle from the crowd.

Brent gives a serious nod. "*Charlotte's Web* is a sad book, but it's a really *good* book. And I don't know if you know this, but people sometimes want to ban it because the animals can talk in it. It's not real, Mrs. Swanson. I know animals can't talk. But Charlotte really is a very smart spider. That's all."

Farah takes the kids back to their parents to a smattering of applause.

Anderson frowns and reaches for the microphone. "It's all well and good to cherry-pick a few heartwarming stories, but some of these books lack any redeeming qualities." He rifles through the pile of books Noelle has laid out on the table behind her. "Like this one." He shakes a copy of *The Sign of the Olive and the Dove.* "It's subversive. Anti-government. Dark and dystopian."

My skin heats. My pulse spikes. I'm not going to let this stand. I can't.

I take a step forward. Quinn yanks me back.

"You promised," she hisses.

From their spot along the side wall, Ivy and Merry are pinning me twin death glares. I raise my hands in surrender and lean back against the wall. Meanwhile, Holly has snatched both the book and the mike from Anderson's hands.

"You cannot be serious. Jackie Samuel's Resistance series teaches empathy, courage, and optimism. It shows teenagers the power they have when they band together and raise their voices, the way Farah and her classmates did yesterday with their peaceful counter-protest. This series inspired me to go to law school, to work to make things better instead of lying down and accepting the status quo." Her voice shakes with feeling and fierce conviction.

I struggle to keep my composure in the face of Holly's

impassioned defense. My heart hammers against my ribs as she cradles my mother's book. She's articulated exactly what Mom hoped to accomplish with the series. The desperate need to tell her the truth of who I am claws at my throat, but I swallow it back. Not here. Not now.

Just then Vicky Swanson stands up, whispers "excuse me," and runs out of the room. When she streaks past me, I'm sure I see tears in her eyes.

I follow her out into the hallway. As I do, just before the door swings closed, I hear Anderson discrediting Holly's position as "emotional," but I know Holly can take care of herself. Right now, I'm not so sure Vicky Swanson can.

She stands facing the window, her thin shoulders shaking. I take two mugs of hot cocoa from the table Merry's Sweets has set up outside the meeting room and walk over to join her.

"Hot chocolate?"

She turns to me, swiping tears away from her cheeks. After a long moment, she takes the outstretched cup. "Aren't you …?"

"I'm Jack Bell. I started this mess by putting those books in your library box."

She frowns. "No, my Pete has it right. I started this mess." She looks at me wryly. "Pete, he's my husband, you know what he said to me?"

"I don't."

"He said I deserve a lump of coal in my stocking for kicking up such a fuss." She shakes her head and sips the hot drink. "He didn't even come tonight. Said he couldn't in good conscience. Said Douglas would be appalled."

"Who's Douglas?" Something tells me to ask the question gently.

"He's our son. Was our son. He overdosed during his freshman year at college. I've spent fifteen years wondering what I could have done to prevent it. Maybe I shouldn't have allowed video games. Or rap music. Or certain books. What could I have done so that he'd still be alive?"

My chest tightens. "I'm so sorry. And I obviously didn't know your son, but I know this much: what happened wasn't your fault."

She sets the cup on the windowsill and wrings her hands, staring out at the glowing holiday lights on the square. "Maybe, maybe not. I don't ever want another parent to go through that. But then, I hear those kids talking about what the books mean to them, and I think, maybe I'm wrong?"

I study her. She's brittle and maybe a bit difficult. But her experience has shaped her. I see a woman in need of connection, community, and care, and I make a snap decision.

"I'm helping Noelle plan a Banned Books Bingo for the Bookmas Event. Why don't you join the committee?"

"Oh, I don't—"

"I think you should. It might ease your concerns about

some of the books. And we could use someone with a green thumb to help Ivy with the flower arrangements."

She blinks behind her glasses then musters up a smile, just as the doors open, and the crowd pours out, making a beeline for the treats.

"I'd like that."

CHAPTER 23

SUGAR AND SPICE AND A GINGERBREAD MISHAP

Holly

Once again, I'm late to a Christmas non-date with Jack. I run into the old barn on the hill behind the MacIntoshes' farmhouse, noting even as I rush how festive Merry and Quinn have managed to make the space. The barn's interior glows with strands of white lights crisscrossing the exposed beams overhead. Fragrant fresh pine boughs hang from the walls. Twenty folding tables—one for each team—stand in four rows of five. Each table is covered with a snowflake-patterned tablecloth and holds a large tray containing gingerbread pieces, bowls of colorful candy, and piping bags of royal icing in red, green, and white. The air is thick with the warm, spicy scent of fresh gingerbread mingled with the sweet notes of peppermint and vanilla.

"Sorry," I mouth as I drop into the empty chair next to Jack at our table and he shakes his head at me. "This time, I have a rock-solid excuse," I whisper.

From the front of the barn, Merry frosts me with a stern look. I give her a sheepish smile. Before she can chide me for being tardy to the gingerbread house competition, two more latecomers slink in through the open barn doors. She turns her glare on Tabitha and Anderson. Whew, at least I'm off the hook. The fact that I took the shortcut past Starlight Lake and got ahead of Tabitha's Mercedes on the one-lane road to the barn helped.

"So sorry. We had an important legal matter," Tabitha explains as they slide into seats at the sole empty table.

"Me too," I say to Jack under my breath. "Important legal matter."

While Merry reminds us of the rules, I whisper, "The three of us just came from the judge's chambers. Vicky backed out of the case. She doesn't want to press charges against you anymore, so Anderson had no choice but to drop the lawsuit."

He gives me a wide-eyed look, disbelief warring with hope on his face. "Really? It's ... over?"

"It's over."

Merry rings the cowbell in the front of the room to signal that it's time to start building. The room buzzes with energy, competitors chatter excitedly over the clink of candy being sorted into separate dishes.

"So you don't have to stay in town," I tell him as he

picks up two slabs of thick gingerbread. The thought of him leaving and me returning to my loft makes my chest feel hollow, a bit cold. I cover my reaction by counting out a row of peppermints.

I can feel his eyes on me as he says, "But if I do stay, Rule 1.8 won't apply anymore, right?"

That hollow in my chest fills as heat flares in my belly. "That's right," I murmur.

"In that case, I think I'll stay."

I raise my head and meet his eyes, opening my mouth—to say what, I'm not yet sure. Before I can form a sentence, he pops a sugar-covered gumdrop in my mouth.

"We shouldn't be eating the building materials," I tell him.

He responds by shoveling a handful of mini marshmallows into his own mouth.

I giggle, then take a look around the room. By the door, Anderson and Tabitha, wearing matching intense frowns, are working furiously. They place candies with surgical precision. The Morgenthals are crafting an elaborate Victorian mansion, with Ryan guarding the candy from his diabetic husband's sneaky hands. Ariana and her group of stitch and bitch knitters are making an adorable storefront with intricate patterns in the glass-sugar window panes.

I look back at our table and notice a thick squiggle of white goo covering part of the roof of our structure—which is supposed to be the inn. "What's this?"

"I thought we'd make it accurate. That's the temporary tarp."

"Oh, of course. It needs fake snow." I throw a handful of white glittery sugar on top of the icing.

I'm surprisingly unfazed by the fact that our entry is, by far, the worst looking. It's embarrassingly bad, but I'm not embarrassed.

I pipe some shingles on the mess of a roof. "So you're staying?"

"I'd like to. If that's okay with you."

"I'd love that." My hand shakes and the icing squirts wildly down the front wall of the house. I meet his gaze. "But you should know, I'm still going to be really busy."

"Even though the case has been dropped?"

"Well, Anderson isn't giving up."

"I don't understand."

I angle my body away from Tabitha and Anderson's table and lower my voice. "The judge signed the order dismissing the case against you with prejudice." I sigh. "But Anderson already filed a new case. He's seeking an injunction to prevent the library from going forward with the Banned Book Bingo."

"But, how can he do that?" A piece of toffee cracks in half in Jack's hand. So much for our front door.

"He can't, not really. He filed on behalf of Citizens Upholding Normal Traditions. But with Vicky's change of heart, that's not a real party. He's obviously working with

James Woodlock's group, which doesn't have standing to bring a case in state court."

I examine our inn. The walls are sturdy, if uneven. While I work on striping the roof with alternating rows of green and white spiced gumdrops, Jack creates a passable wraparound porch using pretzel sticks as the railings. It's actually not half-bad, especially given our shaky start.

I pass him a chunk of green fondant and we start crafting tiny wreaths for the windows. His expression is taut, and I know it's not because he's concentrating on the decorations.

"Jack, I've been appointed to represent the library. He's not going to get his injunction."

Relief flits across his face. "Still, I'm definitely staying now."

"Because of the lawsuit?" My hand stills.

"Holly, look at me."

I do, and the air between us heats.

"I'm staying to be with you." His eyes are dark with an intensity that has nothing to do with gingerbread construction. The familiar warning bells in my head fall silent as I remember there are no more rules keeping us apart. "But even if I didn't want to stay for intensely personal reasons, there's no way I'd leave you to fight Anderson and James Woodlock alone. Even if all I can do is rub your feet and carry your law books."

"How very Darcy of you," I say, my voice an unfamiliar rasp.

He lowers his head and I lean forward to meet him. As his mouth covers mine, my hand slips off the table, smashing into our gingerbread inn. Peppermints and gumdrops fly off the structure and roll across the plank floor.

I peek up to see heads turning to watch as our creation continues its slow-motion collapse. The porch implodes with the crack of breaking pretzel sticks. Merry raises an eyebrow from the judges' table, while Anderson and Tabitha exchange knowing smirks. Ariana and the knitters titter behind their hands. But Ryan shoots me a sympathetic wince as he shields the Victorian to protect it from flying pretzel pieces. Josh uses the distraction to steal a red licorice whip from their candy pile.

"I don't think we're going to win," Jack whispers against my mouth.

I dissolve into laughter, gasping for air and kissing him all at the same time.

CHAPTER 24

RUN RUDOLPH RUN

Jack

Saturday morning, Holly pads into the bedroom before the sun to wake me with a gentle shake and a cup of coffee.

"It's time to get up," she whispers.

I reach over and click on the bedside lamp. Even though Rule 1.8 is in the rearview mirror, we're still sleeping separately, taking turns on the cramped couch. I plan to change that soon—tonight if possible. But last night, she made us go to bed both separately and ridiculously early to prepare for the Run Rudolph Run 5K Fun Run, sponsored by Rudy's Bar.

I rub my eyes and squint at the clock.

"It's five-thirty." I flop back on the bed and roll over.

"Right," she chirps. "Up and at 'em."

"The race doesn't start for two more hours."

She grabs my arm and tries to drag me upright. "And you need to warm up your muscles and eat something."

I wrap my arms around her waist and pull her into the bed. "I have some ideas for warming up my muscles," I say, rubbing the scruff of my beard along her cheek.

She squeals, pretends to struggle, and then nestles against me. I drop a line of kisses along her jaw down to her collarbone and smooth her hair out of her face. Her chest rises and her eyes go liquid as she looks up at me.

My heart thumps in anticipation and I lower my head.

But she says, "We really should conserve our energy until after the race." She rolls over and slips out of the bed. "Come on. Up."

She flips on the top light and jogs out of the bright room, her knees high.

When I join her in the kitchen, she's crouched on the floor threading jingle bells through the laces of her trail shoes. I lean against the island and give her a curious look. "How seriously do you take this fun run?"

She stands up and dusts off her hands. "Here's the deal. I ran cross country in high school and college. I have never placed outside of the top two runners in my age group and gender."

"In this run?"

"In any run," she clarifies.

"Huh."

She lifts an eyebrow. "I'll remind you, I wasn't planning to run this year. This was *your* idea."

"I didn't realize you were so competitive about running," I explain.

"Wait, you *do* run, right?" she asks, reaching past me for the refrigerator. She takes out the giant Greek yogurt parfait she prepared last night, hands me a spoon, and digs in.

I dig out a bite of mostly granola, trying to avoid the yogurt. "I run," I tell her.

"Well, what's your mile time?"

"I don't time myself."

She blinks at me as she tries to process this clearly foreign concept.

"You don't time yourself," she muses.

"I run in nature. I'm not in a hurry. I'm taking it all in."

She puts down her spoon and the yogurt bowl to take what I can only imagine is a centering breath. "Okay, that's fine," she says. "This is your run. We can just do it for fun. It's through the woods. We'll take it all in. It'll be nice."

I can tell she hasn't quite managed to convince herself. I lean over and plant a kiss on the crown of her head. "It will be. You'll see."

Holly

When we get out of the car in the parking lot at Santa's Cellar, I see Anderson and Tabitha warming up by the check-in tables. When I told Jack I run competitively, I neglected to mention that so does Anderson, or that every year I took first or second place, so did he. It was one of the things we enjoyed doing together, pushing each other further, faster.

But I'm sure I can ignore my competitive instincts. Probably. Maybe.

Jack wanders around the parking lot, slapping people on the backs and chatting while he gnaws on a sesame bagel like it's not destined to sit in his stomach like a rock. I sip some water and watch out of the corner of my eye as Anderson gets his hydration vest in place and fills the pockets with gels—complete overkill for a 5K, but that's Anderson. I notice Tabitha is wearing a pair of white racing shoes. They're obviously brand new, shiny, spotless, and stiff. The cranberry pink details pop against the dirty snow. The shoes are an interesting choice for a trail run, I think, as I hear my name and turn to see my sisters, Noelle, and Dad with a group of guests from the inn.

I jog over and Noelle reaches out to unpin the number I've pinned crookedly to my shirt. She straightens it, repins it, and gives it a pat. "There."

"Thanks. Are you guys running?" I ask.

"No, some of the guests are doing the 1K walk," Dad says.

"So we're here for moral support and to cheer on you and Jack. Run like the wind," Ivy adds.

I grimace. "Jack wants to run it for fun. Take it all in."

My family exchanges knowing looks.

"Did you tell him?" Merry wants to know.

"Tell him what?"

"That you only play to win," she says.

"I can do it," I protest. "Run for fun."

My dad snorts and rubs his hands together. "This was definitely worth getting out of bed for."

Nebula turns off the pre-race music and tells all runners to report to the starting line. I dismiss my family with a wave of my hand and run off to find Jack so we can line up. We jostle into place near the middle of the pack just as Dawn fires the starter's pistol.

And we're off. The middle school students have lined the trail with bright red ribbons so there's no chance of veering off the path in the snow. We jog along, the sound of jingling, jangling bells filling the air as dozens of pairs of feet hit the frozen path.

Jack runs easily, his limbs loose. His form is solid, but he looks around and keeps up a steady stream of conversation as we run. Up ahead, I see Anderson sprinting as Tabitha strides a pace behind him. I resist the urge to pour on the speed and nod along to Jack's observations.

As we're chugging uphill past the waterfall, he comes to

a stop and reaches for my arm, maneuvering out of the path of the runners. "Look!"

I glance toward the thicket where he's pointing. "What am I looking at?"

"A purple finch."

I follow the line of his finger and see the pinkish bird. I smile and take a deep breath of chilly mountain air. Jack's right. This is a richer, fuller experience than running the trail as fast as I can, searching for nothing more than a personal best.

We're about to return to the path when I spot a velvet brown doe and two babies blinking at us. "We have company," I say.

He turns, spots the deer, and then brushes a hot kiss over my cold lips. I forget all about the race and kiss him back harder. He backs me against a tree, the bark rough against my neck, and braces an arm on each side of me, boxing me in.

That's when I hear the moan. Faint, and low.

He pulls back. "Was that you?"

I shake my head no.

He pulls me upright and we run around the curve in the trail. Tabitha leans against a boulder, her right foot hovering a few inches above the uneven ground. She moans again.

We run over to her.

"What happened?" I ask.

Her face is tear-stained and twisted with distress.

"I tripped. Rolled my ankle."

Jack squats to inspect her ankle. She inhales sharply and winces when he touches it. Even through her running tights, it's obviously swollen.

"Can you put any weight on it?" he asks.

She tests it and yelps. "No. I think I sprained it."

"Where's Anderson?" I look around for him. But even as the words leave my mouth, I know the answer. He's probably crossing the finish line by now. He left her here.

A red stain blooms across her cheeks and she averts her gaze. "I think he went for help."

The silence that follows is heavy until Jack says, "You're going to get cold standing here. Holly and I can help you up the trail."

"No, please, go ahead," she grits out from between clenched teeth. "I'll be fine."

"Tabitha, don't be ridiculous. Let us help you," I tell her.

She exhales and nods. Jack and I position her between us, and she loops one arm around each of our shoulders. She hops on her good foot and we support her as we inch our way up the hill toward the finish line, waving runners and eventually walkers around us. Our bells jangle out of rhythm as we walk, hop, walk.

By the time we cross the finish line, Anderson's already posing with his winner's medal, Nebula's spinning post-race tunes, and the raffle prizes have been drawn.

We maneuver Tabitha to the first aid station and wait with her as the paramedic on duty proclaims she has a severe sprain. Two pain killers later, she's hobbling around in a walking boot. The parking lot is basically deserted. And Anderson's long gone.

"We missed the free beer. Can I buy you one back in town?" She asks in a hopeful tone.

"You really don't need to," I begin. Then I realize she needs a ride.

Freaking Anderson *left* her here. He's no doubt well on his way to his traditional post-race brunch at the North Pole Social Club. Tabitha made this bed and there's a part of me that wants to let her lie in it, but I can't. I just can't.

"A beer sounds great," I tell her.

CHAPTER 25

BETRAYAL, PARTY OF TWO

Jack

After a round of Frosty ales at Rudy's, we tuck Tabitha into a Sober Sleigh and walk up the hill to town. It's started snowing again, fat flakes drifting down in the cold air. Holly laughs and brushes them off my beard.

"I feel sorry for her," she says more to herself than to me.

"Who? Tabitha?"

"Yeah."

I consider this. She's a likable enough person, but I don't actually like her. "She's the DA, though. Couldn't she shut Anderson down if she wanted to? Why doesn't she rein him in—just because they're dating?"

Holly shrugs. "Maybe. Probably. Anderson can be

charming, when he wants to be. And he's a pro at making a girl doubt herself." She makes a *tsking* sound. "I should know."

I'm even more confused. "Because you worked with him, you mean?"

She stops in her tracks, right in front of the candle shop. "No, because I was engaged to him until he screwed my boss in a closet."

Now I stop. We're blocking the door, and an apologetic mom with three little ones in tow and a big bag full of candles hovers in the doorway, trying to get out of the shop without running into us.

"Sorry," we blurt in unison and move a few feet away.

Once we're clear of the entrance, I reach for Holly's arm and turn her to face me. "You were *engaged?* To Anderson?"

She stares unblinkingly at me. "Yeah."

"You didn't think to tell me?" Anger flares in my gut. I don't know if I'm pissed because it could have impacted my case or because I feel like a fool. The former is less pathetic, so I roll with that. "There's no *ethical rule* about letting your client know you used to bone opposing counsel?"

Her eyes go wide and her face tightens. "I beg your pardon?"

I know I crossed a line, I know I should apologize. But I don't. "You heard me."

"No, Jack. There's no ethical rule about that. And you're right, I should have told you. To be honest, this whole town knows. Every single resident heard the story of how I opened the closet looking for swizzle sticks during the office Christmas in July party and found the man I planned to marry undressing our boss."

Her voice is steady but the faintest tremor runs through her body as she speaks. Tears fill her blue eyes but don't spill over. She's keeping it together through sheer force of will.

She goes on, "So I guess I just assumed the whole world knew, including you. But now you do know. And it clearly didn't impact my ability to represent you. So, you can … you can … go deck your own halls!"

She wrenches her arm away and sprints up the hill, kicking up new snow in her wake. Regret lands like a punch to the gut before she's taken three steps, but I can't undo the damage. All I can do is watch her race away from me. As she goes, I'm struck by two thoughts. One, she was really holding back during that 5K—she's fast. And two, I believe I've just been told to go eff myself in the most festive way imaginable.

Holly

By the time I storm into the cottage and gather my laptop and a change of clothes, my anger is spent and all that's left is my humiliated hurt. I can't believe I was falling for Jack—strike that, I *fell* for him—and he could be so callous about the most painful event in my past. I feel like a fool. Like a sucker. Like I never even knew him.

I run out of the guest cottage straight to the inn. I'm almost to the back door when I realize I'm running into my mom's arms—but they aren't there. That's when the tears start afresh, and I fling the door open and plop myself down at the kitchen table. Noelle must have heard the door slam because she flies into the room, takes one look at me, and backs out, calling for my sisters.

By the time she returns with Merry and Ivy in tow, my head is cradled in my arms on the table and I'm fully sobbing. Ivy pulls out the chair next to me and rubs my arm.

"Shhh. Holls, what happened?"

I raise my head and tell them the whole pathetic story, pausing only to wipe away the snot that leaks from my nose like a faucet.

Noelle takes one look at me, draws her shoulders back, and starts barking orders like a general. "Holly, you march yourself into my bathroom and take a long, hot shower. Merry and Ivy, get yourselves dressed for a night out and find something for your sister to wear."

"Um, okay. Where are we going?" Merry asks meekly.

Noelle gives her the stink-eye. "Tonight's the Jingle and Mingle at the Social Club. Now get moving."

"Yes, ma'am!" They scurry off.

Noelle wraps her arms around my shoulders. "Honey, I'm so sorry. Nobody should ever make you feel that way. And I know you know better than to let them, but you trusted Jack. That's why this hurts. After a night out with your sisters and a good night's sleep, you'll be ready to talk to him about it. Trust me on this."

I do trust her. Mom would have made hot chocolate and told me to listen to my heart, then helped me analyze every word Jack said until we uncovered the true source of his anger. But Noelle's not my mom. She's my friend, and her practical approach is exactly what I need right now. I stand up and hug her.

"Thanks, Noelle."

She strokes my sweaty hair. "Of course. And you'll sleep in our room tonight. Your dad can spend the night on the couch at the guest house."

"Oh, no, Noelle. Don't do that."

She gives me a knowing grin. "Jack's going to need a shoulder to cry on, too. And your dad has the broadest shoulders in town."

I laugh weakly and shuffle down the hall toward the bathroom she shares with my dad. As I push the door open, my phone dings in the pocket of my fleece. Curious whether it's Jack texting some lame apology, I take it out and check the display.

No, the background search I did on Clean Books, Healthy Minds is ready. I hit the download button and the documents populate on my phone. I turn on the water to get hot and lean against the glass-walled shower, scrolling through the documents while I wait. When I get to the article titled "Son of Acclaimed Author Scuffles with Book Activist James Woodlock at Funeral" I almost drop my phone on the tile.

Jack Bell is Jackie Samuel's *son?* Jackie Samuel was a pen name for Veronica Bell, mother of two boys, Jack and Samuel, whose names she used for her pseudonym. Jack and James Woodlock got into a fight at his mother's funeral? And *I'm* the one who withheld information? *I'm* the one who should have opened up?

Of all the tinsel-wrapped nerve. I put my phone on the counter, rip off my clothes, and step into the hot shower. The water pounds against my shoulders as the truth washes over me: I shared my most painful memory but he kept this massive secret. The feeling builds until I think I might explode from the sheer force of the betrayal. I tip back my head and let out a scream that would scare Krampus himself.

CHAPTER 26

THE MORE YOU PUSH, THE MORE SHE'LL PULL

Jack

Holly's already been to the cottage and left. I can tell as soon as I walk in. The air smells faintly of that spicy/citrus scent that I identify only as "Holly." That, and her laptop bag is gone. I'm sure she couldn't get out of here fast enough after the way I treated her.

I stand in the doorway to the bedroom and give the king bed a baleful look. Had it really only been this morning when I'd had plans to take Holly into that bed and spend hours exploring every inch of her body? And now, I'll be lucky if she ever speaks to me again.

I kick around the house, feeling sorry for myself for a while, then try to decide whether to open one of the bottles of wine or take a shower first. I raise my arm and sniff my armpit. Definitely shower first. But there's no law against shower wine, I think. I'm headed to the wine fridge when someone pounds a heavy fist on the front door.

That does *not* sound like Holly. Not unless she's even angrier than I thought. I crane my head to look out the window over the kitchen sink and see Nick Jolly standing on the porch. There are three or four figures behind him, but I can't make them out in the snow. I square my shoulders. If Nick's here to ice my cookies, I'll take it like a man.

It's not until I'm opening the door that I realize the Christmas near-swears are rolling off my tongue like I'm a native. So, I'm chuckling when the door swings open. One look at Nick's thundercloud face and the laughter dies in my throat.

"Son, I don't know what you did, but whatever it was, you messed up good," he announces as he strides inside, bringing a gust of frigid air and the smell of wood smoke with him. "Now, where's the bottle opener?"

He drops a case of Frosty lager on the kitchen island. Titus, Enrique, Enzo, and Christian MacIntosh file in behind him, stomping snow from their boots on the welcome mat, shedding their coats, and brushing melting snowflakes from their faces.

I hand Nick the opener and check the porch before shutting the door. "What, no Morgenthals?"

"They're flying out to California to celebrate an early Hanukkah with Ryan's mother. The holiday starts on Christmas this year, and Josh has his heart set on playing

Santa, so they'll do their holiday out there, stay to watch Lois's roller derby championship, and then they'll fly back here on Christmas Eve."

"Ryan's mother plays roller derby?"

"Correct." Nick pops the caps off a half-dozen bottles and passes them around.

Once everyone is clutching a cold beer, Nick raises his in my direction. "So, what'd you do?"

Several beers later, we're camped out in the living room and I've spilled the entire story about Anderson abandoning Tabitha on the trail, how that resulted in my finding out that Holly and Anderson had been engaged, and how I didn't handle it with a lot of grace.

Enzo squints at me. "Never liked that guy."

"Who? Jack?" Enrique points in my general direction. It's a fair question, frankly.

"No. Ander*son*."

"Nobody liked Anderson," Nick says evenly. "At least, not for Holly."

There's a general chorus of agreement. I'm about to ask Nick the most important question of the night, when Titus's cell phone trills several times. He glances down at a text. Scrolls. Scrolls some more. Then he lets out a low whistle and passes it to me.

Delphina sent him a rapid-fire series of texts:

JACK BELL is the son of Holly's favorite YA novelist. He let Holly talk about her AT LENGTH and NEVER mentioned that fact.

Oh, and he got into a FIGHT with that Woodlock jerk AT HIS MOM'S FUNERAL.

Don't you think he should have told her???

Don't you????

My stomach hits my knees. I hand the phone back and drain my beer.

"I've never seen Delph use so many capital letters or question marks in a text," Titus observes as he hands the phone around the room, letting everyone read it for himself. "I think you might be in more trouble than you realize."

"I'd say that's a certainty," Chris says, very judge-like. "I'm sure Holly thinks your former relationship with James Woodlock was at least as relevant to the case as her former relationship with the ADA."

My stomach lurches again. Enzo passes me a beer.

"Better text your girl back," Enrique counsels Titus.

"Should I defend Jack?"

"No!" the others shout in one voice.

"Thanks," I say in a dry voice.

"There's no reason for Titus to bunk in the dog house with you," Nick tells me. "Why didn't you tell her who you are?"

"I have … reasons," I say lamely, knowing how hypo-critical I am. I deliberately kept my past from Holly and lit into her for not spilling her history with me.

"What are they? We can't help you unless we know what we're up against," Nick said.

I jerk my head. "You're helping me? Even though Holly's rightfully angry with me?"

"Well, that depends on how good your reasons are."

So while Titus thumbs out a response to Delphina, I try to explain the mess I'm in.

"My brother Sam and I inherited our mom's publishing, well, empire. But after the scuffle at the funeral, her estranged husband, who still has a minority seat on the board, convinced the rest of the board members that I wasn't mature enough or responsible enough to run the company. So they voted to put the ownership into a trust run by Roger—that's our evil stepfather—and give me until the end of the year to prove myself. Sam's been working for the company under Roger's thumb while I've been on this redemption tour. I've been distributing banned and challenged books all across the country and filming it as I go. The idea was to create a record of me defending my mom's legacy and so many other books against censorship in a low-key way without drawing any attention to myself." I hang my head. "So when I went and *got arrested*, the last thing I could do was say, by the way, I'm Jackie Samuel's younger son, the one who's a screwup."

There's a long silence. Then the judge grunts. Nick nods.

"What? What does that mean?"

Enzo looks from the judge to the innkeeper and then at

me. "You need to call your brother and get him up to speed. Right?"

"Yup," the judge tips his bottle in Enzo's direction.

"Okay." I don't know how involving Sam helps, but I'm fresh out of ideas, so I'll take what they have. "And what about Holly? Should I try to explain or apologize or—"

"No," Nick cuts me off. "I'm going to tell you what Holly's mom said when the rest of us wanted to figure out a way to make Holly see that she shouldn't marry Anderson. Carol said the thing about Holly is the more you push, the more she'll pull. It's just a fact."

I stare at him. "So, what does that mean? What do I do?"

"You wait her out," Nick tells me.

"Wait?"

"Wait." He pauses, burps, and adds, "You can, if you like, drink while you wait."

Wait. The word sits heavy in my chest and goes against my every instinct. I try to fix things, even if most of the time all I do is make them more broken. But considering how well that approach has worked out so far, maybe it's time to try something different. So I'll wait.

CHAPTER 27

JINGLING, NIX THE MINGLING

Holly

Ivy and Merry veto my choice of outfit and makeup, instructing me to take off several layers of the former and add several layers of the latter. I'm numb enough that I allow them to take over, which results in my walking into the North Pole Social Club wearing a silver sequined minidress and a smoky eye. Delphina and Quinn, who were tasked with holding down a table until we arrive, both do double-takes.

"You're fire," Quinn tells me.

"Holly Jolly, who knew you had this side?" Delphina cracks.

I tug at the top of the strapless dress Merry lent me and give them both a look. It's a minidress on my sister. I have five inches on her, so it's more like a long tube top on me.

"Just so you know, I am not dressing for the male gaze. I did this for me."

"Sing it, sister," Delph agrees.

"She did it because she was completely zoned out while we got her ready," Ivy explains.

"And one more thing," I add, pointing around the red velvet settee. "I only want to jingle. Not mingle."

The social club's annual party is known for its strong singles vibe. The absolutely last thing I want to do is flirt.

"Noted," Merry says. "Yes to dancing, no to flirting. What about jangling?"

I give her a blank look. "What?"

"The signature drink tonight is the Jingle Jangle Peppermint Espresso Martini," she explains. "Because the coffee will make your nerves jangle."

"Oh. Oooh. Bells, yeah to jangling!"

"Did you just say … bells, yeah?" Delph paints me with a pained look.

I start to laugh, then I remember where I heard the phrase and the laugh turns into a growl. Ivy flags down a tuxedoed waiter. "Quick, we need five Jingle Jangles." She jerks a thumb at me. "It's an emergency."

The waiter gives us a wide grin. "Got it."

When the drinks arrive, I'm just finished catching everyone up with the whole saga. We thank the server profusely. He must hear enough of my sad tale to understand our mission because he says, "I'll just keep them coming."

Quinn rewards him with a bright smile. "Perfect."

We raise the martini glasses in a toast. "To jingling," Merry says.

"And jangling," Ivy adds.

"And us," I declare.

We throw back the drinks and I can tell the Jingle Jangle is going to be dangerous. It's sweet, creamy, and has a kick.

"I can't believe Anderson left Tabitha in the woods," Delphina says.

"I can't believe Jack didn't know about Holly and Anderson," Quinn counters.

Ivy gapes at them. "I can't believe Jack is Jackie Freaking Samuel's son!"

Merry nods her agreement. "That is the biggie."

"It is, right?" I say. "Like that's a huge secret to keep from your girl—lawyer."

"Girl—lawyer? Is that like a Girl Friday?" Delph wants to know.

I feel the blush creep up my neck. "I was going to say girlfriend, but that's not what I am. Was. Am?"

"Ouch. You've got it bad. Come on, time to jingle." Quinn pulls me to my feet and the five of us hit the dance floor.

We form a tight ring and dance our booties off, our hips swaying and our hair flying, as the bass reverberates in my chest. The sequins on my borrowed dress catch the lights, sending tiny sparkles across the floor. Whenever someone tries to encroach on our circle, Merry tells them our coven isn't interested in men except when we need a human sacrifice. After the third time, the news must spread because nobody will meet our eyes, let alone approach us.

We collapse back on the settee for another round of martinis. The red velvet is hot against my bare legs. Above us, silver tinsel dangles from a crystal chandelier drip, and everywhere the scents of peppermint, alcohol, and coffee mingle with perfume and sweat emanating from the dance floor. It's both gross and exactly what I need.

"How'd you come up with the human sacrifice bit?" I ask Merry.

"Aunt MJ."

"That tracks."

Ivy sips her fresh drink. "You do know why you're so mad at Jack, right?"

"Because he's a jerk?"

Merry shakes her head. "No. Because you opened up about your deepest hurt and he kept quiet about his biggest secret."

I sit with this for a minute. Then I say, "Which is very unfair."

We drink in silence until Ivy clears her throat. "Only you don't like to talk about Anderson because you're trying to protect yourself from reliving a really crappy experience. But Jack kept his identity a secret to protect his family business, not himself."

She's deduced this motive from another article that I

showed them about the Jackie Samuel publishing empire. Apparently, Jack has until the end of the year to convince the board he can be trusted with the business. She thinks he was afraid if he told anyone who he was, the news of his arrest would spread. And maybe she's right, but I was his girl—lawyer. He should have told me.

I'm about to make this point, when Delphina says, "Unlike some people who shall remain nameless but whose initials are AWC, Jack hurt you because he's loyal, not because he's a disloyal snake."

She has a point. But still. Regardless of Jack's motive, he did hurt me. I drain my glass. "More jingling!"

We hit the dance floor until our feet hurt and we need to cool down. Then we weave our way through the throng of gyrating bodies and return to find five more martinis arriving at the table just as we do.

I'm definitely feeling the effect of the drinks, so I sip this one more slowly. "So what should I do?"

"Accept it," Merry says with conviction.

"*Accept it?*" I do not like this advice.

"Accept that whatever you have with him is imperfect. He broke your trust. But that doesn't mean you throw out the whole man," Ivy expounds.

Quinn shrugs as if to say, well, you *could*.

Delphina says, "I think what your drunk sisters are trying to say is that sometimes people deserve second chances. Anderson did not. Maybe Jack does. Maybe he doesn't. Just let it play out."

"Just let it play out?"

"Just let it play out," she repeats.

Her words spin around me like snowflakes. Or maybe that's my head spinning. It's hard to tell. Part of me wants to argue, to demand a plan of action, to take charge the way I always do. But maybe Delph is right. Maybe sometimes you have to let things unfold naturally.

"Okay," I finally say.

"Okay." She gives my hand a squeeze.

We finish our drinks, the world's best waiter pours us into a Sober Sleigh, and I fall asleep on the way home with my head lolling on someone's shoulder.

BANNED BOOK BINGO

Jack

Holly successfully avoids me all week. According to Noelle, she's returned to her loft. So I have the cottage to myself and, frankly, it sucks. But I keep my beery word and resolve to wait. Luckily, I'm so busy working with Noelle and Farah to pull the banned book bingo event together that waiting is only incredibly difficult, not impossible.

On Friday, Judge MacIntosh denies Citizens Upholding Normal Traditions' request for an injunction. This means the banned book bingo can go forward as planned. When Holly calls to let Noelle know, Noelle puts her on speakerphone so she can to deliver the good news to the whole committee. The sound of her voice breaks my resolve and I move toward the phone to say—I don't know what. *Something.*

But then Vicky rushes in from the parking lot with a worried expression.

"What's wrong?" Noelle asks.

"I was waiting for Ivy to pull in so I could help her carry in the snowball hydrangeas for the flower arrangements. James Woodlock just showed up with some of his people. They're setting up a tent in the parking lot. I heard them say that the order Holly got last week has expired, so by the time she finds out about the tent, court will be closed until Monday. They're going to throw snowballs at the kids coming in for bingo. Isn't that awful?" She's aghast.

Holly's voice crackles through the speakerphone. "I don't think pelting children with snowballs is even remotely upholding normal traditions," she says dryly. "But, since we know what they're up to, I'll draft the order now. Mrs. Swanson, I'll need to bring over an affidavit for you to sign, basically swearing out what you overheard. Will you do that?"

Vicky's chin trembles, but she nods. "Yes," she says in a clear voice.

I know she still feels some responsibility for Woodlock showing up in town, but she's going all out to redeem herself. She even meets Farah for tea every afternoon to talk about a different banned book.

"Great. I'll be over as soon as I can."

"What if you can't get the order to the judge before court closes for the weekend?" Vicky frets.

"I know how to get ahold of him after hours," Holly assures her.

I help Farah wrap books for prizes while Ivy and Vicky decorate the tables. Noelle and Merry set up the hot coffee station. We all ignore the hammering we can clearly hear ringing out in the parking lot.

When Holly calls to let Vicky know she's on her way, I wander outside to wait for her. Yes, I want to steal a minute or two alone with her. But mainly, I don't want Woodlock to hassle her. She may not want my protection, but she has it.

The afternoon has grown downright cold. The wind cuts through my heavy jacket, chilling me to the bone. I stamp my feet to warm them up and breathe into my bare hands. Finally, I see Holly's car pulling into the closest open spot and I walk out to meet her.

A guy with a long mane of brown hair elbows Woodlock, who turns to track me as I cross the lot. He picks up a bullhorn from a folding table and holds it up to his mouth.

"The depraved son of a depraved woman," he crows, walking directly toward me.

Holly locks eyes with me for an instant that feels like an hour. Then she backs away, behind her car. I continue to walk. I don't look at Woodcock or acknowledge that I've heard him.

"A broken family with broken values. That's the Bell legacy. That's what Jackie Samuel will be remembered for."

His taunts don't get to me the way they did at Mom's funeral. For one thing, I'm not out of my mind with grief. For another, James Woodlock needs some new material, these insults are all recycled from the last time he confronted me. And maybe most importantly, I think Holly's recording this interaction. The possibility that she is makes it easier to unclench my jaw, let my hands hang loose at my sides, and keep my steps measured and steady as I walk past him.

I reach Holly's car, still ignoring Woodlock's shouts.

"Hi," I say.

"Hi." She lowers her phone.

"Thought I'd walk you in."

"I'd like that." She gives me a smile.

We walk inside in silence. But I already have that smile tucked in my pocket.

Holly

My legs finally stop shaking while I'm going over the affidavit with Vicky. When I heard James Woodlock screaming at Jack, it triggered a huge flight response in my body. Standing my ground, even behind the car, and filming the confrontation took all my resolve. I wanted nothing more than to flee. My hands trembled so badly I wasn't sure the video would be usable. But watching Jack maintain his composure, seeing him choose peace over pride, steadied something in me, too.

The last time I checked, the video I uploaded to social media with the hashtags #jackiesamuelson #notnormal #banbookbans had gone viral. I made sure to tag Sam Bell, the Jackie Samuel Companies, the Board of Directors, and, for good measure, Tabitha Waterson and the County District Attorney's Office. Granted, a lot of the shares seemed to be young women focusing on how hot Jack is. I mean, they aren't wrong, and a share's a share.

I'm hopeful this clip will show how much Jack's grown. Maybe it will help demonstrate that he has both the passion and the temperament to protect his mom's legacy. If nothing else, it's a start.

I'm about to slip my phone back into my pocket when it rings. The display shows the call is coming from the DA's office. I steel myself for more of Anderson's steaming hot reindeer poop and answer the call.

"H. Evelyn Jolly."

"Holly, it's Tabitha."

I'll take Tabitha over Anderson any day. According to Chantal, Tabitha dumped him the Monday after the 5K and had his office moved to the smallest, windowless room right near the break room. All he does is complain about people microwaving popcorn and roam the halls looking forlorn.

"Hi, Tabitha. This isn't a great time I'm in a bit of a rush. I need to get an emergency order over to Judge MacIntosh before the end of the day."

"Doubt you'll need it."

"Oh?"

"I saw your video."

I pause. It's possible the video could be helpful in demonstrating Woodlock and Clean Books, Healthy Mind plans to harass the crowd the way he harassed Jack. But the DA wouldn't ask for the order on the library's behalf. Would she?

She goes on. "I forwarded it to Judge MacIntosh and he had the courthouse tech people enhance it. That's clearly Anders in the background coaching the protesters. The enhanced video shows him telling them to throw icy hard snowballs at children and appears to show him passing out twenties to the protesters. I assume that's why you tagged me?"

Uh, no. I don't have the faintest idea what she's talking about. Not even a ghost of a hint of an idea. But it sounds like something Anderson would do. And leave it to him to be bold enough to do it out in the open, where anyone could have seen him. It's true what they say about criminals: they aren't very smart.

"Yes, exactly," I say.

She exhales. "Thanks for sending it along. His termination is going to be messy, no doubt. But knowing Anders, he'll land on his feet." She doesn't sound happy about this.

"Unfortunately, that's probably true," I commiserate.

"At least he'll be out of my hair—and yours."

"And what about James Woodlock and his people?"

"Judge MacIntosh called the county police personally. They'll oversee the removal of the tent and will escort Clean Books, Healthy Minds out of town before nightfall."

"Okay, then."

"Anything else?"

"I think we've got it covered. But I hope we'll see you tomorrow at the event." I surprise myself by extending this olive branch.

Tabitha's acceptance is the most Tabitha thing ever. "Of course, the district attorney's office is a firm supporter of the First Amendment right to disseminate and receive information, including that contained in books."

"Of course," I say. Then end the call fast before I laugh at her nerve.

I turn around to see Jack watching me. "How much did you hear?"

"Enough," he says, the corner of his mouth quirking up.

"So, my work here is done."

"Will I see you tomorrow?"

I nod. There's a lot I want to say. Too much. But this isn't the time. Or the place.

CHAPTER 29

CHRISTMAS EVE

Jack

I'm nervous as I slip into the Candlelight Chapel. The place is packed, as I'd been warned it would be. I scan the sea of heads until I spot Holly. Her long blonde hair is braided into some sort of complicated design and piled on the top of her head. Her neck is bowed as if she's reading something or looking at her lap. The candlelight catches the gold in her hair, and my chest tightens. I stride down the aisle and slide into the pew next to her.

She turns and her blue eyes light up. "You made it."

"I told you I would."

She nods. We haven't seen each other since the day before Banned Book Bingo. That clip she filmed went viral, like really viral. So the library was packed with book influencers and legal commentators during the event. It was great for the town and even better for the cause. But it meant she and I never connected that day.

And then, the board asked me to fly straight back to Florida. Sam had circulated the video and the clip of Noelle praising my efforts to some library committee on C-SPAN. Who knew anybody watches C-SPAN? Apparently the members of the board of the Samuel Companies are big fans, because they voted overwhelmingly to give us control of the company effective January 1.

The lone no-confidence vote was Roger, no surprise there. But we've already hammered out a deal to buy him out as soon as the trust lapses. He'll be out of our lives and Mom's legacy in a week.

All good news, but it's kept me in Florida. Holly and I have texted and video chatted. She declared it the modern equivalent of the epistolary themes in Austen's *Emma*, but as far as I'm concerned it's a poor substitute for being able to reach out and touch her. This thought reminds me that I can do exactly that, so I do. I rub my thumb across the underside of her wrist and she sears me with a look that makes a bead of sweat run down my brow. Even in the sacred quiet of the crowded chapel, surrounded by flickering candles and soft, instrumental carols, the electricity between us crackles. She wipes the sweat away with a knowing look.

The service is probably beautiful. I wouldn't know. Finally, after two and a half eternities, we're released into the snowy, starry night. I keep my head down and dodge the well-wishers. Those I can't completely avoid, get a curt greeting.

"Jack, you're being rude," she whispers.

"Wrong," I whisper back. "All these people who are interfering with my most important goal are being rude."

"And what goal is that?"

I press my mouth against her ear and murmur my plans for the evening. She blushes the deepest red, so red she matches her coat. Then she grabs my hand and starts to run, pulling me along behind her.

"What are you waiting for?" she cries over her shoulder.

We race into the cottage, breathless and laughing while we take off our wet shoes. Her cheeks are flushed from the cold. I brush melting snow from her neck and she shivers. Then the air shifts and our laughter fades. She looks up. I follow her gaze. Someone has hung a sprig of mistletoe over the doorway. I lean down and kiss her hard. Her lips part and the smallest moan escapes.

I'm done waiting. I scoop her up and carry her across the room to the bedroom. I kick the door closed behind me and lay her down on the bed with supreme care, drinking in the sight of her. Her hair is coming loose from its elaborate braid, and her eyes shine in the dim light. At long last, we're here, in the king bed where I've slept, where she's slept, but where we've never slept together.

Tonight, I can't promise that anyone will be sleeping.

CHAPTER 30

CHRISTMAS DAY

Holly

I wake early, before the sun, in a tangle of sheets in the arms of the man I love. A smile plays on my lips as I extricate myself, creep across the room, and ease the door open silently.

It must have snowed all night. The windows are frosted with lacy patterns and the room is cold. I light a fire and start the coffee. When Jack pads out of the bedroom, he crosses the room to plant a minty toothpaste kiss on my cheek.

"Merry Christmas."

"The merriest," I say, handing him a mug of gingerbread latte "coffee" with candy cane foam.

He takes a sip and his eyes pop. "Tell me the coffee shop isn't open today."

"It's not. Delphina taught me how to make it."

He smiles into his cup. "This is a nice surprise."

"It's not the only one." I can't wait any longer, so I pull open the drawer built into the island, where I hid his gift days ago. I hand him the small package.

He unwraps the silver patterned tissue paper so carefully, so slowly, that I have to stop myself from ripping it out of his hands and doing it myself. He swallows hard when he holds up the glass ornament. Inside, a miniature bookcase holds a tiny set of Jackie Samuel's Resistance series novels.

"So you can celebrate your mom's legacy every Christmas."

"Holly, I—," his voice breaks and he trails off.

"Wait, you have another one." I pull him over to the couch and push it aside to reveal a large box. He sets the ornament aside and gets to work on the box. When he sees that his gift is his very own little free library, he roars with laughter.

"I wanna keep you out of jail," I explain as I hand over his third and final gift.

"Well, this is a book," he says, turning the wrapped hardcover in his hand.

"D'uh. I thought you could put it in your library."

He tears off the paper to reveal a copy of *Pride and Prejudice*. I watch him flip it over and read the inscription.

To Jack,
You're definitely more of a Darcy, with the gooey
center of a Bingley.
Yours,
Holly

He smiles up at me. "They're perfect. You're perfect."

Then he disappears into the bedroom. Curious, I follow him.

He lowers himself to the floor and reaches under the bed to pull out a large package wrapped in simple brown paper. He rests it on the bed, and gestures for me to unwrap it.

"But how—?"

"Elves. Santa's helpers. Fine, your sisters."

I giggle and tear one corner of the paper. As I work the paper off, I reveal a corner of the painting and instantly recognize Pedro's distinctive style. But after I remove all the paper, I'm speechless. This isn't just any painting. It's *What Remains Beautiful.* The lines, the colors, the broken being mended—it all hits me just as hard this time as it did the first time I saw it.

"Thank you."

"Judge MacIntosh told me it resonated with you." He tucks a strand of hair behind my ear.

"It did. Does," I correct in a soft voice before pressing my face into his shoulder, overcome by it all.

He wraps his arms around me and holds me, surrounded by paper and ribbons and all our beautiful, broken pieces.

A NOTE FROM MELISSA

Dear Reader,

Whew, writing this book was a journey. If you read *Home for Christmas in July,* you may remember that I dedicated it to "anyone who needs a reminder that light triumphs over darkness."

Fast forward half a year and that someone was me. While I was writing this book, my mother's cancer recurred, we thought she beat it, we learned she didn't, and, on October 31, 2024, she passed away.

At that point this book was mostly written. And for a while, I thought that might be its permanent state. But eventually, I returned to the manuscript. And then set it aside. Lather, rinse, repeat. Until eventually, Holly and Jack's story grew louder than my own, and I turned this book over to them.

At the end of the day, this holiday rom-com mystery is

a story about secrets, celebration, brokenness, and repair. More than anything it's about finding the beauty in the impermanent, the imperfect, and the incomplete—during the holidays as well as the rest of the year.

Love,
Melissa

THANK YOU!

Thank you for reading *Booked for Christmas*. If you're new to Mistletoe Mountain, you can read Nick and Noelle's story in *Home for Christmas in July*.

All my books. If you're new to my books, you have a lot of choices! My website melissafmiller.com contains an up-to-date list of *all* my books.

USA Today bestselling author Melissa F. Miller majored in English literature with concentrations in creative writing poetry and medieval literature and was stunned, upon graduation, to learn that there's not a robust job market for such a degree. After working as an editor for several years, she returned to school to earn a law degree.

After practicing law for fifteen years, including a stint as a clerk for a federal judge, nearly a decade as an attorney at major international law firms, and several years running a two-person law firm with her lawyer-husband, she turned in her bar card to make up stories instead.

Now, powered by coffee, she writes full time from the

Pennsylvania home she shares with her family and their cat and dog. (The cat's in charge.)